BOND & BOOK
The Devotion of "The Surgery Room"

"Do as you please."

"I can lend you my assistance one more step of the way."

hat
eck...?
’s not
alker,
osy?”
“I’m not really one of the station’s lending books. I belong to Hana.”

"If you're unfaithful to me...I won't ever forgive you. I swear."

Her voice was as sweet as ever, even as she sulked.

An image floated before me of Princess Yonaga, her jet-black hair spilling smoothly down over her shoulders, her slender body clad in a glamorous kimono. She turned her pale face toward me and stuck out one red lip dramatically.

What can I say? My girlfriend is adorable!

"I'm not cheating. I would never do that. I mean, come on, you're my soul mate, Princess."

"......"

"Listen, I love you."

I gently stroked the elegant indigo cover with my fingers, and Princess Yonaga seemed to shudder a little.

"I'm a book, so...all I can do is watch over the person I care about."
"Musubu, thank you. I'll take good care of you!"
"I wanna go on an adventure!"

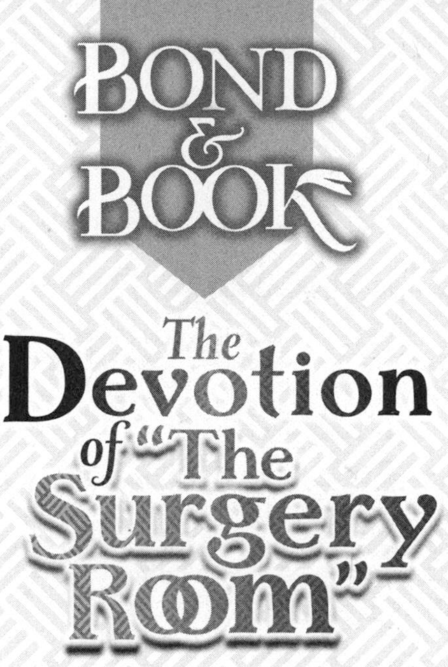

Mizuki Nomura

ILLUSTRATION BY
Miho Takeoka

New York

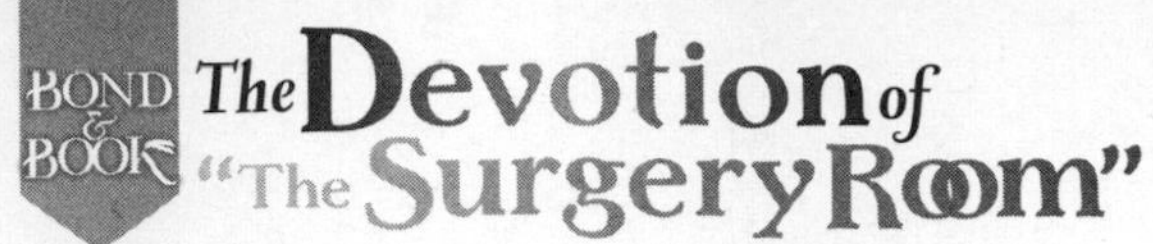

MIZUKI NOMURA

Translation by Nicole Wilder
Cover art by Miho Takeoka

This book is a work of fiction. Names, characters, places, and incidents are the product of the author's imagination or are used fictitiously. Any resemblance to actual events, locales, or persons, living or dead, is coincidental.

MUSUBU TO HON. "GEKASHITSU" NO ICHIZU

First published in Japan in 2020 by KADOKAWA CORPORATION, Tokyo.
English translation rights arranged with KADOKAWA CORPORATION, Tokyo through TUTTLE-MORI AGENCY, INC., Tokyo.

Yen On
150 West 30th Street, 19th Floor
New York, NY 10001

Visit us at yenpress.com • facebook.com/yenpress • twitter.com/yenpress
yenpress.tumblr.com • instagram.com/yenpress

First Yen On Edition: September 2021

Yen On is an imprint of Yen Press, LLC.
The Yen On name and logo are trademarks of Yen Press, LLC.

The publisher is not responsible for websites (or their content) that are not owned by the publisher.

Library of Congress Cataloging-in-Publication Data
Names: Nomura, Mizuki, author. | Takeoka, Miho, illustrator. | Wilder, Nicole, translator.
Title: Bond and book, the devotion of "The Surgery Room" / Mizuki Nomura ; illustration by Miho Takeoka ; translation by Nicole Wilder.
Other titles: Musubu to Hon. "Gekashitsu" no ichizu. English
Description: First Yen On edition. | New York, NY : Yen On, 2021.
Identifiers: LCCN 2021023513 | ISBN 9781975325732 (v. 1 ; hardcover)
Subjects: CYAC: Books and reading—Fiction. | Magic—Fiction. | Mystery and detective stories. | LCGFT: Novels.
Classification: LCC PZ7.N728 Bk 2021 | DDC [Fic]—dc23
LC record available at https://lccn.loc.gov/2021023513

ISBNs: 978-1-9753-2573-2 (hardcover)
978-1-9753-2574-9 (ebook)

10 9 8 7 6 5 4 3 2 1

LSC-C

Printed in the United States of America

CONTENTS

Book 1

A Happy, Happy Day for *Pippi Longstocking*

I heard a voice as I passed through the station gates.

"Please take me to Hana!"

The voice rang eager and strong as it repeated its appeal.

"I have to get back to Hana no matter what! Please!"

There was a shelf stuffed full of old books tucked into a corner of the train station, the kind from which anyone could freely borrow. I was out running an errand for my mother after school, but following the desperate plea of the charming voice, I paused and slowly approached the bookshelf to pick up one of the volumes.

On the cover, darkened with age, was a picture of a girl with freckles and braids, wearing socks up over her knees and big floppy shoes. She held a monkey in her arms.

I placed my hands on *that girl* on warped, yellowed pages and peered at the book through the thick lenses of my glasses. I grinned.

Then, in a secretive whisper, I asked, "So *you're* the one who was calling for help, huh? Nice to meet you. I'm Musubu Enoki. Perhaps I can be of assistance?"

For as long as I've been aware, I have somehow been able to hear the voices of books and converse with them. The voices I hear in the local library whisper gently, those in small used bookshops are laid-back and mellow, and books piled up in the new-releases section of big bookstores chatter with excitement as loudly as the chirping of recently hatched birds.

Hearing the voices of books is part of my everyday life, not all that different from the hustle and bustle of other people passing me by. However, every once in a while, I stop in my tracks like this, to lend an ear to their stories and talk with them.

I was certain that fate had brought me to this book, too.

"I'm not really one of the station's lending books. I belong to Hana. When Hana was seven years old, she went to a bookstore with her father. When our eyes met, we both knew it was fate. She asked her father to buy me, and she took me home with her."

So I ended up taking the book home with me.

Back in my room, I set it down on my desk and inquired about its situation again, and the book began to cheerfully tell its story.

The title on her (the voice belonged to a girl) cover was *Pippi Longstocking*. The author was Astrid Lindgren, a Swedish writer of children's books. She wrote the Children of Noisy Village series and the Kalle Blomkvist series, as well as many other famous books.

According to her: "I was the first book Ms. Lindgren published, which means I'm her oldest daughter."

It tells the tale of the greatest girl in the world, who takes her monkey named Mr. Nilsson and a suitcase full of gold coins and moves all by herself into the Villa Villekulla, a house covered in weeds. Chronicling the daily life of a girl with long stockings and oversize shoes, the book is packed with the sorts of adventures children long to have, and it spins a tale that is simply "silly and thrilling."

"Hana was a real crybaby and a scaredy-cat. She cried in her room a lot, like the time she got detention for refusing to eat the tomatoes in her school lunch, or the time she got a nosebleed from getting hit in the face during a game of dodgeball, or the time her mother told her she couldn't watch TV before finishing her homework and turned off her favorite program, *Masked Magical Girl Maids*. But whenever she read me, she would stop crying. She'd even smile and giggle. Hana always said she wanted to be 'just like Pippi.' Whenever she was feeling lonely, I would sleep in bed with her. When she felt anxious, I would go to school with her. Once, when she passed the exam to get into middle school, she even told me she hadn't been nervous because 'Pippi' was right there with her. That made me so happy!

"Hana loved me, and I loved her, too. I thought we'd be together forever—"

I sat in my chair and nodded along as I listened to the disheartened book's narration.

The question was, How did Hana's most precious thing end up on the train station's lending shelf calling for help?

The answer was that one day, when Hana was in her first year of middle school, she had forgotten the book on a station bench.

"Hana had been feeling down all morning. There was no school that day, and she packed me and some ginger cookies she had made into a small paper bag and set off on a little trip. But somewhere along the way, she got off the train, maybe because she was sick, and sat on a bench for a very long time doing nothing at all. Occasionally, she would hang her head and let a few tears fall or rub her eyes or blink a lot... I'm sure something sad had happened. Usually, she would read me, and I would lift her spirits, but that day, she didn't even pick me up. She left me there on the bench, paper bag and all."

After that, the book had been picked up by one of the station attendants.

At first, Pippi was unfazed, certain that Hana would come back for her soon. But Hana never reappeared, even when her ginger cookies had gone totally stale.

"That wasn't a train station Hana usually used, and she seemed spaced-out and sick that day, so she must not have even known where she lost me... If that's not it, then maybe something happened to her..."

She didn't know why Hana hadn't returned. Eventually, it became clear that nobody was coming back for her. The cookies were thrown out, and she was placed on the lending shelf, where she drifted from place to place in the hands of unfamiliar borrowers.

The book couldn't say exactly how much time had passed since then.

Her pages were yellowed, and her cover was quite worn.

"I waited in that place day after day, calling out to everyone who passed me by, asking them to take me to Hana. You're the only one who ever answered, Musubu. Thank you."

"I hope you'll be able to see Hana again."

"Me too."

Her voice brightened and became cheerful again, like a burst of light. I pictured the girl with the freckles and braids breaking into a smile, and I felt myself grinning right alongside her.

Ah, she really loves Hana. I'd like to get her back to her owner.

Okay then, I'll do what I can to help her. After all, I am a friend to all books.

The first order of business was to write down all the information that Pip (as I decided to call her) could give me about her previous owner:

The girl's full name was Hana Higuchi.

She was in her first year of middle school, or maybe older.

She was part of a three-person family with her parents.

She commuted to her private middle school by train.

Her school uniform was a gray blazer with a checkered skirt and a dark-red ribbon.

I looked up the uniforms of nearby private middle schools and had Pip take a look at them, but we didn't find any matches.

"And you don't even know the name of the station near Hana's house?"

"...No, sorry."

Hmm, this might be a tough one.

I crossed my arms in my swivel chair and mulled over the situation.

Fine. I guess I'll try asking the one upperclassman I can always count on.

I went to see him the next day during lunch.

"Again?" He opened his eyes wide. "Musubu, you're really nice to books, huh? How about setting up a one-stop shop for them, instead of helping them individually? I can't think of too many high schoolers who have your ability, so you'd probably do good business, don't you think?"

"I'll consider it as soon as you can tell me how to get the books to pay for my services."

"Got me there."

There on the leather sofa sat third-year student Haruto Himekura, smiling in amusement.

Haruto was tall, handsome, and so cool that people called him the Campus Prince. In actuality, his mother was not only the head of the school board, but also the head of the wealthy Himekura clan, one of Japan's foremost families. Haruto was her oldest son and a resplendent aristocrat.

Normally, someone like him would have nothing to do with a plain, bespectacled commoner like me. It was that "special skill" of mine that got us talking in the first place. Haruto was the only one in school who knew I could hear the voices of books.

We were chatting in the luxurious conference room in the music hall, which towered over the rest of the school grounds. The hall was a modern-style building with a domed roof, used mostly by Seijou Academy's Orchestra Club. The club was known for counting many professional musicians among its alumni, as well as prominent politicians and businessmen. Haruto had been serving as the orchestra club's director since his first year at the school, as is apparently tradition among the eldest sons of the Himekura family.

Once, Haruto told me his mother had said he could join any club he desired and that she wanted him to do something he liked. But Haruto had been set on orchestra from the start. His mother's atelier occupied the top floor of the building, and as a child, Haruto visited often, so he developed an attachment to the place. He had never missed a single concert and always aspired to be part of the orchestra—that's what he'd told me anyway.

He had seemed so cool as he smoothly rattled off the story. We truly were from different worlds.

The reception area of the music hall really was incredible. Parts of it split off to form private lesson compartments, while the rest was dedicated to the impressive conference room.

Beside the leather couch stood a marble table and an amber-clad sideboard lined with endless rows of medals won in various orchestra competitions. It might have been even more impressive than the principal's office. Though I'd never actually gone to the principal's office.

From where I sat, Haruto, who was relaxing in this opulent hall as if it were his own bedroom, seemed as though he could get everything and do anything he desired.

While he would counter that there were lots of ways in which his family obligations constrained him, I imagined he had connections just about everywhere. He could undoubtedly gather valuable information simply by being in the right place with the right people.

In other words, I was sure that if anyone could find Hana Higuchi's whereabouts, it was Haruto. The best I'd managed was looking up her name online, and I hadn't found anybody who even seemed as if they might be a match.

"Well, I think it's going to be difficult with only her name to go on," Haruto said. "It would be hard enough to find her if she were a celebrity or a criminal, but you said she's just a normal middle school girl. And the name Hana has been in the top twenty most-popular baby names for a while."

"I'm sure I can figure something out with your help, Haruto." My glasses slipped down my face as I pressed my hands together in supplication.

Haruto flashed a cheerful smile that would have thrilled any of our female classmates. "All right, but I've got a request for you in return, Musubu."

"So I heard that first, he was just touching their arms and tapping on their shoulders, but eventually he moved on to rubbing backs and running his hands across hips!"

"Right, yeah, those areas are kind of borderline, so even the girls getting touched wonder if they should let it go."

"Mm, that's the really sly part about it. But he's definitely toeing the line. It's almost criminal. That teacher is a pervert."

After school, I found myself in the social studies reference room, listening to the chronological tables and glossaries lined up on the conference table.

There was a rumor going around that Mr. Takekawa, the Japanese history teacher, was sexually harassing his female students. He often conducted private tutoring sessions in this reference room, so I had been tasked with questioning the books that resided there about what was really going on.

Haruto always asked for something in return whenever I needed a favor, with a bright smile to boot. I didn't mind much, though, since I felt awkward about always requesting things from him.

I was having difficulty hearing the books, who had all started talking at once. Their voices were blending together, and I couldn't make out a word they were saying.

"One at a time, please."

I tried to lead the discussion forward, but—

"All right then, I'll go!"

"Okay, listen to what I have to say!"

"I'm first!"

—they all started talking over each other again.

"That jerk Takekawa likes girls who seem inexperienced. He gets extra turned on by serious girls who bear his assaults in silence."

"His tastes are so obvious. He only brings skinny girls here, the kind without any meat on them at all."

"You'd think it would be more fun to touch girls who were a little plumper."

"Mm, like the world history teacher, Mr. Obana, who gets excited by voluptuous older women. Other men's wives, in particular. They've got to be great."

"Agreed. Ieyasu Tokugawa's stable of concubines was full of divorcées, you know. Leave it to the man who united the country to have taste."

"Nobunaga Oda also showed favor to the widows of the Ikoma clan and their servants. He even made them bear his children."

"In comparison, Hideyoshi Toyotomi only went for young virgins. But he liked rich girls. He said there was nothing better than the ones who lacked refinement."

"Hang on, I thought all of Hideyoshi's concubines were also hostages?"

"So they were other men's wives!"

"Ieyasu also went for young girls later in life."

"And we can't talk about Nobunaga without mentioning Ranmaru Mori."

Ah geez, this conversation is getting off track.

"Excuse me! Could we leave this discussion about the concubines from the Warring States period for another time and get back to the sexual harassment allegations regarding Mr. Takekawa, please?"

"I'm telling you, he's guilty!"

"He's a handsy old man!"

"He starts out by patting them on the shoulder, then goes around rubbing backs—"

"Please don't all speak at once! I'm taking notes—slow down!"

They went on and on.

It was evening by the time I made it home.

"Whew, I'm wiped."

I dived onto the bed, still holding my schoolbag, and buried my face in my pillow with my glasses still on.

How should I report this to Haruto, I wonder...? Can I just say Mr. Takekawa is guilty of harassing those girls and leave it at that...?

While I was thinking it over, the clear voice of a girl called out to me, filled with concern.

"Are you all right? Musubu, you look exhausted!"

From where I was lying, I turned to face my desk and smiled. My glasses slipped down my nose again.

"Yeah, an upperclassman just asked me to handle something for him," I replied. "Oh, and I'm doing my best to find out about Hana."

"Thank you. But don't work too hard. If it looks like you're making yourself sick, I'm going to have to do a handstand and walk around backward, you know."

"Ha-ha, I'd like to see that."

"All right, let's give it a go!"

"Wait, you can do that?"

"Put me on the floor, then do a handstand and walk backward. If you do that, it'll look like I'm walking on my hands, too, right?"

"Uh-huh… Yeah…"

"Hana also used to do handstands and play around, 'just like Pippi.' But one time, she fell on her head and got a bump."

"Hmm… It seems like I might get a bump, too, so I'll pass."

"Oh, too bad."

Pip mumbled with seemingly genuine disappointment, then quickly returned to her bright, bouncing voice.

"Hey, I've got an idea—you should try reading me. Hana would always stop crying and cheer up when she did! C'mon, Musubu, read me!"

I smiled as I pictured a cheerful girl with freckles and braids, wearing long socks and big, floppy shoes, her eyes sparkling as she spoke to me.

It really seemed as though my mood would improve if I gave her a read.

"Thank you, but—"

I can't read you here.

I was about to tell her that, when—

"Cheater..."

* * *

—I heard a voice so cold that it instantly raised the hairs on my neck and sent icicles down my spine.

"I won't forgive...infidelity..."

Cherubic but clear as ice, the voice wound its way to my ears from inside the bag I had tossed aside on my bed.

"Cheater...cheater...cheater...cheater...cheater...cheater..."

Oh crap. I meant to leave my bag in the living room, but I was so tired, I forgot.

"Huh? What? Who's there?" Pip asked in surprise.

"Uh, well—"

As we spoke, I could hear the other voice growing even colder, chilling me to the bone.

"Cheater, cheater, cheater... I'll curse you, I'll kill you, I'll dance on your grave—"

"Sorry! Pip, you wait here!"

I flew out of the room holding my bag and ran downstairs to the living room on the first floor.

My mother stuck her head out of the kitchen. "What's wrong, Musubu? You're making a racket. Dinner's almost ready."

"Got it."

Brushing her off, I opened my schoolbag. Peeking out from between the textbooks was the slim paperback I always carried around with me. Dressed in an artsy cover, it was elegant, charming, and terrifying—

"Musubu, I won't let you cheat on me... I'll burn that book and sprinkle her ashes from a tall building. That'll teach her for speaking with my Musubu. Or maybe I'll chop her up page by page and boil her down to pulp in a cauldron, or stick a needle through each of her letters, or scribble over all her words with a red ballpoint pen, or punch holes through each of her corners and thread string through them and have horses tear her to pieces by pulling in four

different directions. Or perhaps I'll pour sulfuric acid all over her cover, make her fall apart so you won't have a chance of reading her. Or throw her to some goats and have her chewed up and eaten alive. Or what about cursing you so that acid falls into your eyes? If I did that, you couldn't stray from me again. That's how grave a sin infidelity is. I absolutely cannot sanction the turning of another book's pages right here in our home. So I curse, curse upon curse, absolutely curse you! I won't let you cheat on me!"

"Wah! I'm not cheating! I'm sorry—I'll come apologize later, so just wait here for a little while."

Cold and cute and ruthless and extremely jealous—Princess Yonaga continued to curse me feebly behind my back as I set my precious copy of her on top of a sofa cushion and rushed up to my room.

"Musubu, who was that? Is she angry you brought me up here?" Pip seemed worried.

I scratched my head in embarrassment and fixed my glasses.

"Uh, well...she's like how you were to Hana. She's the book I'm destined to be with... We can't ever be separated... Frankly, she's my girlfriend."

"Wow!" she exclaimed in surprise. "This is the first time I've ever met someone whose sweetheart was a book!"

I don't doubt it.

There were plenty of people who loved books, maybe even more than was healthy. A few might have said they were married to their books or something. But not many humans were in a monogamous relationship with a single book.

There's a long story behind my relationship with Princess Yonaga. But that aside, thanks to the envious princess, I couldn't take any books other than textbooks into my bedroom.

"I think she loves you a little too much, Musubu. She seems like

CURSE
CURSE
CURSE

she would kill you and the other book if you were unfaithful to her. Her murderous rage made me shiver!"

Hmm...she did say she was going to boil Pip in a pot or throw her to wild goats...

"It's scary to have someone threaten me like that... But I guess you must really love her, too, huh? How wonderful."

"Ah-ha-ha..."

Whenever I read another book, I had to secretly turn the pages behind Princess Yonaga's back, and I always felt really guilty about it. She caused all sorts of problems.

I felt my cheeks flush at Pip speaking of my relationship with the princess so passionately.

"Let's forget about my situation and get back to Hana. Can you tell me any more about her? What she looked like, how she passed the time in her room, any outings you went on with her? Anything would help."

She launched into a delightful monologue as soon as I asked the question.

"When Hana was young, she would imitate Pippi by braiding her hair in two pigtails. She also begged her mother to buy her long socks that came up over the knee. She would put her tiny feet into her father's shoes and smile and declare that she was 'just like Pippi.' And just like Pippi, one time she coated the floor in flour to roll her cookie dough, which made her mother angry and almost caused Hana to cry. 'This book is teaching you nothing but bad behavior,' her mother scolded. She tried to take me away, but Hana squeezed me tight to her chest. 'I'll be good, so don't throw my book away!' She started bawling while defending me. Then she decided to run away from home with me."

"Run away?"

"Just as far as the neighborhood park."

I guess that's usually about how it goes when kids run away.

"The park had a slide that looked like a plesiosaur with a hollow inside, big enough to hold a child. She squatted there and held out

until about eight o'clock at night. It was winter and very cold, so the tip of Hana's nose was bright red and dripping snot. But even so, she held me close and told me we'd always be together. I told her, 'I feel the same way—we'll be together forever and ever.' Eventually, her father came looking for her and took Hana back home."

"You're not going to throw Pippi Longstocking *away?"* Hana had apparently asked.

"No, I'll ask your mom to leave the book alone."

"Really?"

"I promise."

"Thank goodness."

Pip said Hana smiled all the way home. She must have been relieved to the very bottom of her heart. When her father asked, *"Hana, you really love that book, don't you?"* she grinned even wider as she answered:

"Yeah! I love her soooooo much!"

What a great story… I'm glad everything worked out.

But more importantly, that story holds a clue.

"I imagine city parks with plesiosaur slides are pretty rare. I bet it would come up if I searched."

I quickly looked it up on my phone, and—

"Aha!"

—I got a hit, a photo of a slide designed to look like a green plesiosaur holding out its long neck with its head bent toward the ground.

"How about it? Look familiar?" I asked, showing Pip the picture.

"Yeah! That's the slide! No doubt about it!" she answered with glee.

"Great!"

I pumped my fist in celebration.

"It's not that far from here, so we can get up early tomorrow and go look."

That night, I went over the results of my investigation into the sexual harassment allegations against Mr. Takekawa. I typed out everything I had heard in the reference room, sent Haruto an e-mail, and went to bed early.

When I went to say good night to Princess Yonaga, whom I had left in the living room, she started muttering threats in her cherubic voice. **"Unfaithful boy... I'll curse you... You won't know what hit you... I'll summon a plague... Everyone except the two of us should just die..."**

A palpable chill seemed to radiate from the elegant indigo-blue cover. I couldn't help but shiver.

Ah...this is going to be bad. But...I can't do anything about it except wait until the thing with Hana is resolved and then try to win back her favor.

"Good night, Princess Yonaga. I love you," I replied, then went back to my room.

The next morning—

I left my house two whole hours earlier than usual.

"I might be able to see Hana soon!" Pip said cheerfully from inside my schoolbag.

The park with the plesiosaur slide was five stops past the station where Pip had been left, including one train change. The slide towered imposingly over the rest of the playground, in the exact center of the park. I opened my bag and held Pip in my hands, and then her animated voice flowed.

"Yes! Here! This is the park Hana ran away to! Wow, it brings back memories! Hana sat on that bench and read me one time! She got thirsty while she was reading, so she bought a fizzy lemon

soda from the vending machine and drank it. Then she let out a cute little burp and looked around anxiously, worried someone might have heard it."

"Do you know the route to Hana's house from here?"

"I'll try to remember!"

"Okay, tell me."

"Um, first head left down that road... Turn the corner at the convenience store, then go straight for a while..."

She showed me the route, recalling the days she had been brought to the park while clutched against Hana's chest.

Along the way—

"Which way was it, now? Um...probably this way."

—there was some uncertainty—

"Oh, this looks wrong. I'm sorry, Musubu, go back to where we were before."

—but eventually—

"This is it! This road! There were pretty orange flowers hanging over the wall. The dog that lives at the house over there would stick his face out of the gate and whine until Hana petted him. And I remember that cherry tree! In the spring, it blooms full of pink flowers, and on sunny days, Hana loved to sit underneath it and gaze up at the blossoms. She would stop and stare at them forever. That house over there had hydrangea bushes, and Hana couldn't stand slimy things, so whenever she saw a snail, she would leap with fright."

The closer we came to Hana's house, the quicker words tumbled from her.

My heart also sped up as I searched the sunny residential neighborhood for a doorplate that read HIGUCHI.

Suddenly, Pip shouted, sounding the happiest I'd ever heard her. "Behind that apartment building! That's where Hana lives!"

All right! We found Hana's house.

I jogged around to the back side of the building and was greeted by a construction schedule plastered to a bulletin board that stood in front of an empty lot.

Huh?

Why...?

I stared at the unexpected vacancy for a while, overcome with surprise.

Pip must have been even more taken aback.

The house where she had lived with her beloved Hana had completely disappeared.

"Are you sure there's no mistake? Could it maybe have been one house over?" I asked, holding on to the smallest glimmer of hope.

"No...this is the right spot."

She was despondent, and my heart felt even heavier.

What on earth could have happened to make Hana's home disappear like that?

Just then, an older woman came out of the house next door, accompanied by a dog.

"Excuse me," I said to her. "I was expecting to find Hana Higuchi's residence here. Do you know anything about her?"

I explained that I was a former classmate of Hana's and that I had come to visit, only to find her house was no longer standing.

The woman replied, "Oh, little Hana? My goodness, are you her boyfriend?"

I put together a story on the spot about being Hana's boyfriend—how we'd had a fight and broken up, how I just hadn't been able to forget about her, and how I'd come to see her at home and was shocked to find her place missing.

The woman looked at me with heightened interest, then said something even more surprising. "Hana's parents got divorced, you know. If I remember correctly, I think her mother got custody of her."

Hana's parents got divorced?!

And I suppose they sold the house?

Pip was still silent in my arms.

"Would you happen to have contact information for the Higuchis?"

"I'm sorry, young man. The move itself happened so suddenly that I never had the chance to ask. I'm sorry I can't be of more help," the woman apologized.

"...Not at all." I bowed stiffly. "Thank you very much."

Then Pip and I left the place where Hana's house used to be.

She remained quiet the whole way back to the station.

"We still have other leads, you know. Like Hana's middle school uniform. I bet if we narrow our focus to schools in this area, it'll get a lot easier to pinpoint the right one. Plus, if we consult the real estate agent, they'll probably know Hana's new contact information. I'll ask Haruto about both of those things. I'm sure with just those clues, he'll be able to find Hana for us soon."

"You're right, Musubu. Thanks for cheering me up," she responded brightly, as if trying to encourage herself, but after that, she stayed silent.

Somehow I made it to school on time after visiting the park.

When first period was over, I immediately went over to the third-year classrooms. I had messaged Haruto and told him I was on my way, so he was waiting in the hall for me.

The girls passing us by smiled radiantly at Haruto. They probably felt lucky just catching sight of him, since he was so tall and handsome, not to mention the chairwoman's son. Real high school royalty!

We moved to a spot without any foot traffic, and I reported the developments in the situation with Mr. Takekawa, as well as what I had learned about Hana's case.

As I had written in my e-mail, Mr. Takekawa was apparently pretty slimy.

And as for Hana, it seemed her parents had divorced and moved away, leaving an empty lot behind. Hana had gone to live with her mother.

"Got it. I'll look into the next bit of information for Hana's case. You've really helped me with Mr. Takekawa. I don't want his victims to suffer any public scrutiny, so I'd like to deal with the situation as discreetly as possible."

Haruto's still just a high schooler like the rest of us, but he has to keep up with everything on campus. Must be tough… Then again, I don't think it's in his nature to just watch silently when something bad happens…

"It seems like all of Takekawa's victims were quiet, serious girls," I said, "so I'm sure they'll appreciate that kindness. And thanks in advance for your help with Hana."

Haruto said to leave it to him.

That was enough to reassure me.

Now if only Pip would cheer up, too… Seeing an empty lot where her home once stood must have been horrible.

Besides that, I had a feeling Pip was in quite a weakened state. Her voice didn't really tell the story, but her cover and pages did. Some kind of crumbly dust had even fallen out of her spine once, and her pages were brittle and dry. It made me anxious.

While walking down the hall, I was absentmindedly thinking about how I should repair her when I nearly collided with someone who came around the corner ahead of me.

"Oof!"

"Ah!"

We stopped so close to each other that our faces almost touched.

The girl, dressed in a school-issue T-shirt and shorts, glared at me.

She was slender and beautiful but looked primed for a fight.

Her T-shirt read *First year, Class 6—Sanae Tsumashina.*

She's in the same grade as me.

But she was scowling at me, so I decided to keep my head down and apologize.

"Sorry."

"Watch where you're going."

Tsumashina didn't have any words of apology. She stuck her pretty nose in the air with a snort and then quickly walked on.

Whoa, what a jerk! I mean, I said I was sorry. And what did she do? She just snorted at me! She snorted! I absolutely can't stand girls like her, no matter how pretty.

That's what I told myself anyway. But part of me didn't really buy it—after all, my "girlfriend" was the type of "girl" who wouldn't hesitate to commit murder and then laugh innocently as she looked down at the corpse.

Anyway—I watched as a middle-aged man boldly strode up to Tsumashina and stood close to her.

Isn't that Mr. Takekawa? The man with the heart stained so dark it's practically black, the one the books in the reference room called a perverted bastard and a groper?

Mr. Takekawa is talking to Tsumashina.

Dammit, I can't hear them from here.

Just as I stepped down the hall, intending to feign ignorance and pass them by, the two of them started walking side by side.

This means Tsumashina is in danger, doesn't it? She fits Mr. Takekawa's predilection for serious girls with slim figures. But based on how she glared at me earlier, she seems like she would slap him silly if he touched her. Besides, they're just walking together...

But they're headed for...

"Gah!"

I let out an unconscious gasp when I realized they had gone into the social studies reference room, the very place where I had struggled to sort out the books' discussion just the day before.

That room's bad news!

Really bad news!

I rushed up to the door.

Do I push it open and pretend I came to look for some old document? Or do I observe the situation from here? But if what the books talked about were to happen to Tsumashina...

The books said that first he talks with them, playing the part of an enthusiastic instructor...then he casually pats them on the shoulder or touches their arm, then starts rubbing their backs and hugging them. His targets don't know how to react, so they stare down at the ground, and he relishes watching their discomfort out of the corner of his eye.

"That teacher is a pervert."

* * *

Here I am worried about getting another angry look? I've got to go in there!

"Pardon me—"

The moment I opened the door—

"Dirty old teacher!"

"Augh!"

—I heard Tsumashina's angry shout, together with Mr. Takekawa's yelp of surprise. Tsumashina leaped into the air, driving a fist toward Mr. Takekawa's face. Her slim body flexed, and her solid right cross connected with the direct center of Mr. Takekawa's nose.

He staggered backward dramatically and collided with a shelf stuffed with volumes of reference books, which sent them tumbling down on his head and shoulders.

"It's divine punishment!"

"Hit the harasser with everything you've got!"

"Let's give the perverted bastard his due!"

The falling tomes yelled courageously, and every time they landed on Mr. Takekawa, he yelped in anguish—it seemed especially painful whenever their corners hit him.

As for me, I stood in the open door, watching it all go down in a state of shock.

"What was with that shouting just now?"

"Hey, what happened?"

Other people were gathering behind me.

The avalanche of books having finally ceased, Mr. Takekawa stood back up with a miserable look on his face.

"Owww… Wh-what's wrong with you, Tsumashina? Assaulting a teacher out of the blue?"

Apparently, he had decided to play dumb.

The students behind me looked at Mr. Takekawa, who was staggering to his feet with a big red mark in the center of his face, and Tsumashina, who was still glaring at him in a fighting stance.

"He said that girl is responsible."

"An assault? At school? She may be a girl, but she's scary."

Tsumashina raised her eyebrows in disbelief, somehow managing to look even angrier.

"You had your hands all over me, didn't you?! Perverted teacher!" she shouted.

"That's right, that's right!"

"He touched her arm!"

"He patted her shoulder!"

"He rubbed her back, too!"

"Her waist— Well, he didn't touch that yet."

The books voiced their agreement, but I was the only one who could actually hear them.

Mr. Takekawa made an even more bewildered expression. "Our arms just bumped into each other a little," he insisted. "A-and then you suddenly got all angry."

It seemed he was determined to play the victim, and the assembled students bought every word—

"Oh, screw you! You touched my shoulder and my arm and my back, and you know it!"

Tsumashina furiously stuck to her story, but—

"Well, people do bump shoulders and arms sometimes, you know."

"And teachers are always patting us on the back."

"Isn't she making a big deal out of nothing?"

—her insistence had exactly the opposite of its intended effect.

Tsumashina must have heard what they were saying. Her face stiffened into a look of frustration.

At this rate, she would be accused of assaulting a teacher without provocation, so I spoke up.

"It wasn't an accident," I said. "Mr. Takekawa clearly touched her on purpose. I saw it myself."

Mr. Takekawa shifted his focus to me, as did Tsumashina, who raised her eyebrows in surprise. Both of them were clearly wondering who I was.

* * *

"First, Mr. Takekawa, you said she could tell you anything. Then you patted her on the shoulder. After that, you told her she could depend on you, and you touched her arm."

The truth is that I hadn't actually observed any of this happening myself; I was just repeating what the books had said word for word.

But Mr. Takekawa knew that I knew what he had done. "Wha…?! You— How long were you there?" he stammered.

"Long enough to see *everything*," I replied.

Well, maybe I didn't, but the books did.

"The first two times you touched her could probably be explained away, but rubbing her back was crossing a line," I continued. "And it was when you tried to put an arm around her hip afterward that Tsumashina busted out her right cross, wasn't it?"

Mr. Takekawa didn't say anything. He simply trembled with fear. Tsumashina's expression transformed from disbelief to surprise as she stared at me. And the tone of the students behind me also began to change.

"Mr. Takekawa was sexually harassing her. There's an eyewitness, so there's no doubt about it."

"Oh, ew, how awful!"

Ah shoot, Haruto said he wanted to deal with this quietly, but now word's definitely going to get out…

As expected, Mr. Takekawa's sexual harassment became the talk of the school.

People said there were apparently quite a few other victims, and his misdeeds had been discovered when a certain first-year boy happened to witness him in the act. But the real star of the story was Tsumashina, the girl who had knocked Mr. Takekawa off his feet.

"They say she socked him right in the face with a single punch. So cool!"

"She's beautiful and has a great figure, too. And strong on top of that? I *wish* I was her!"

While the girls praised her, the boys weren't so quick to admire—

"Yeah, she's pretty, but isn't she kind of scary, too?"

"She sure wears a fierce expression… Why would Takekawa make a move on her? Anyone can see she's a land mine."

"I heard she was the one who invited it. One of her friends was a victim, so she decided to lure Takekawa in and expose his evil deeds."

"I understand the sentiment, but she went past heroic and straight into terrifying. I wouldn't want to have her as a girlfriend."

When I passed Tsumashina in the hallway, she didn't seem to recognize me. Her lips were tightly pressed together on her stiffened face, and she walked along with her back held rigidly. It seemed as though the criticism and accusations were weighing on her, their toll evident on her body. Just looking at her was enough to stress me out.

During lunch, I caught up with Haruto in the conference room of the music hall.

He told me Mr. Takekawa had been officially dismissed.

"Thanks to Tsumashina being so conspicuous, none of the other victims seem to have become a topic of conversation. I'm glad for that, but I feel sorry for her, what with everyone gossiping about her and all…" Haruto frowned.

"Can't you do anything about it?"

"I feel really bad for her, but there's little anyone can do except wait for this whole thing to blow over. Though it'd be a different story if something major enough to overshadow the Mr. Takekawa thing would happen. Of course, then we'd likely just have a new problem on our hands."

"We sure would."

There are so many things even an all-knowing prince is powerless to change, much less an ordinary nerd like me. There's nothing I can do. And I doubt Tsumashina even remembers what I look like anyway…

"Anyhow, the Mr. Takekawa incident is kind of a sensitive issue, so it's probably best to keep out of it from here on. I'm having people look into

Hana's whereabouts as we speak, so I should be able to give you a new lead by tomorrow at the latest."

"That'd help me out," I said.

"You don't look all that happy," Haruto remarked. "You really are worried about Tsumashina, aren't you?"

"Well, there's that, but…it's Pip—er, Hana's book. I'm worried about her. She's in bad shape."

Even Pip wasn't sure how many days she had spent at the station's lending shelf. But it seemed as if it might have been much longer than I had originally thought.

Maybe she sounded so desperate when I first heard her because there's some reason why she has to see Hana soon. If that's the case, then I'd better hurry, or she'll…

Haruto listened carefully to what I was saying, a look of concern on his face.

"I'll contact you as soon as I find anything, Musubu."

When I got home, I went up to my bedroom on the second floor and pulled Pip from my bag, then set her gently on the desk.

"I'm sure you're tired from today. You can rest here."

"…Thanks. You're right… I am tired, probably from too much excitement. But only a little. I'm fine, really," she mumbled.

When we had set out in the morning, she had been so happy, thinking she would see Hana soon, but now she sounded defeated.

"Haruto said there ought to be some progress by tomorrow."

"…Yeah."

It seemed as though just talking to me was wearing her down. She had grown more and more depressed since seeing the vacant lot where her home had once been.

"All right, I'm going to take off for a bit."

"…Sure. And, Musubu, thank you for today."

I could tell by her voice when she thanked me that she was still feeling down. Just hearing her made my chest tighten.

I want to get her to Hana.

As quickly as possible—

No matter how far away Hana's moved, I swear I'll bring Pip to her. Even if she's in Hokkaido or Okinawa or somewhere even farther.

"Ah, but…maybe not overseas. I don't have a passport."

No, we don't know whether Hana is overseas or not. We'll figure that out when the time comes.

Filled with grim determination, I balled my fists up tight as I made my way downstairs to the living room.

"……"

The night before, Princess Yonaga had suddenly gone completely silent. Now, sitting beside a porcelain doll on the shelf, the slim, indigo volume was surrounded by an almost-palpable aura of rage. I felt my spirits sink as soon as I laid eyes on her.

Shoot, she's mad. She's really, really mad.

"Uh, I'm home."

I greeted her, feeling as if I was going to break into a sweat. Of course, it didn't go over well.

"……"

"Um, were you bored?"

"……"

"I'm sorry. I didn't think you would like being in my bag with Pip."

"……"

"Besides, she not doing so well, so I didn't want to make her more anxious. She's already apologized for pulling me away from my girlfriend."

"…You told her I'm your girlfriend?"

At last, she answered.

Her tone was brusque; evidently, her mood had not improved much.

"Sure, I mean, you *are* my girlfriend, right?"

I stuck my face up close to the shelf and put on a cheerful smile.

Princess Yonaga went quiet again for a moment, then whispered, **"…Cheater."**

Ah, so she's still suspicious…

"If you're unfaithful to me…I won't ever forgive you. I swear."

Her voice was as sweet as ever, even as she sulked.

An image floated before me of Princess Yonaga, her jet-black hair spilling smoothly down over her shoulders, her slender body clad in a glamorous kimono. She turned her pale face toward me and stuck out one red lip dramatically.

What can I say? My girlfriend is adorable!

"I'm not cheating. I would never do that. I mean, come on, you're my soul mate, Princess."

"......"

"Listen, I love you."

I gently stroked the elegant indigo cover with my fingers, and Princess Yonaga seemed to shudder a little.

"Today I'm going to take my time and read you slowly. Savoring every line."

I moved to embrace her—

"No, don't touch me."

—and was immediately rejected.

"What's wrong?"

Didn't I clear everything up?

"Hmph!"

Ah, just now, she said, "Hmph!" She's so cute!

But the words that followed were as cold as ice.

"Until you completely part ways with her, you may not touch me, turn my pages, or read me at all."

"What, seriously?!"

No matter how I begged her to take it back or how I explained that Pip already had her own soul mate in Hana, she wouldn't budge.

"Hmph!"

Ah, so cute! Come on!

I want to turn your pages! I want to turn them so bad! I want to read you all night long!

But I didn't have her consent. My shoulders drooped in defeat.

During dinner, I set Princess Yonaga on my knee, prompting my exasperated mother to ask if I wouldn't mind putting the book down during mealtimes at least. Ruthless, Princess Yonaga barked from my lap, **"Be my** chair, Musubu. But remember, right now you're not my boyfriend, merely my servant, so you mustn't turn a single page."

When I returned to my room after dinner, Pip seemed out of it. She didn't even notice when I came in.

This was different from Princess Yonaga's deliberate silence. Rather, her presence itself was faint. It felt as if she might fade away and disappear at any moment.

"Pip?" I asked anxiously.

"Ah...Musubu. Welcome back," she answered quietly.

Ever since I had met her, she had given the impression of being a lively young girl of about elementary school age. But now she seemed like a sweet little grandma.

"Musubu, you look sad. Did you have a fight with your girlfriend?"

"...It's fine. Princess Yonaga is always moody."

"But...you seem really down."

Ah crap, I thought I was smiling. Was I not?

"I'm sorry, Musubu."

Hey now, why is she apologizing to me? This is my own fault.

"It's nothing you should concern yourself with, Pip. Princess Yonaga and I are really very close. Just like you and Hana."

I tried to force myself to smile.

I was not sure if I actually succeeded.

Faintly, she said, "That's good."

And then she was silent again.

The next day, I left Pip to rest at home and went to school with Princess Yonaga in my backpack.

"You mustn't read me out here, even with that girl at the house, you know."

Princess Yonaga's prohibition was still in effect, but maybe because she had been lonely at home the day before, she was in a much better mood. I could tell she was in high spirits even if she didn't spell it out.

That made me happy, too, though I was still obviously quite worried about Pip.

I hope Haruto has some good news for me today.

As I gazed out the train window at the passing scenery, it crossed my mind that we would soon be at the station where I had first encountered Pip...

Huh?

I recognized a girl sitting on one of the benches at the station.

She was slender and a little fierce looking—it was Tsumashina.

I guess she boards from this station?

But even when the train stopped and the doors opened, Tsumashina remained glued to the bench with a vacant expression on her face. She didn't move at all.

Maybe she's not feeling well and is taking the day off?

The bell rang to signal the train's departure.

Taking the next train would likely mean being late to school.

When the doors closed and the train sped off, I was on the platform at a station that wasn't mine, walking toward the bench.

I mean, she looks really unhappy. I can't just leave her like this.

"Tsumashina?"

When I called out to her, Tsumashina broke from her daze, eyes opening wide and eyebrows raised in disbelief.

"You again? Why are you everywhere now? Are you stalking me or something?"

What an awful accusation. I was starting to regret getting off the train.

Inside my bag, Princess Yonaga fumed.

"A girl's voice? You're cheating again."

"I just happened to see you sitting there and got off the train to check on you since you looked unwell. I guess you're all right, though."

As we talked, the next train arrived, and the doors opened.

"You'd better go," Tsumashina urged. "Otherwise, you'll be late."

"What about you?" I asked. "You're not getting on?"

"What do you care?" she replied.

"I can't just wander off and leave you alone," I insisted.

Tsumashina turned away in a huff. "What the heck…? So he's not a stalker, just nosy?" she grumbled.

The doors closed, and the train departed.

Well, we're definitely going to be late.

"Could it be that you don't want to go to school?" I asked. "Are people saying stuff to you about yesterday?"

"…That's all everyone's talking about. You must know that."

"Yeah," I mumbled. "I heard."

Even though Tsumashina had been the victim, people were saying all sorts of nasty things about her, like that her reaction was unladylike or that she wasn't girlfriend material.

That has to hurt, no matter how thick her skin…

I couldn't help but pity her.

"…Meanwhile, everyone is just calling you the 'first-year with glasses.' No one really knows your name. Even though you had a lot to say to Takekawa at the time."

"My bad, sorry for being so plain, I guess. Not that I'm demanding your gratitude or anything, but you know, if I hadn't spoken up back then, Takekawa would have played dumb, and you would probably be in trouble for assaulting a teacher."

I puffed my cheeks out a little. *A bit of gratitude* would *be nice.*

"…You're right," she said. "Thank you."

Wow! She actually thanked me!

I suddenly felt terribly embarrassed. "Um, I feel like I kind of forced that out of you," I said. "I'm sorry."

"It's fine. You really did help me."

"Nah—"

"Though it was kinda creepy that you were watching for so long, not to mention that you could rattle off everything Takekawa said to me."

Creepy?

I wanted to tell her that the books had been watching, not me, but that would have sounded crazy on top of creepy, so I couldn't reveal the truth.

"I was so shocked, I froze up… I'm sorry I couldn't stop him earlier."

That excuse would have to do for now.

"It's fine… I handled that perv on my own."

"Yeah, that was some punch." I let my true thoughts slip.

She just glared at me again. "Anyhow, I'm sure you think I'm freakishly strong or that I'm awful and scary. That I'm definitely not the type of girl you'd ever want to date."

"Th-the thing is…"

I admit it: I did think that. But it's because of what happened before *she punched Mr. Takekawa—when she stared daggers at me for almost running into her.*

Wait, I get it now. In that moment, she was wound up because she was getting ready to use herself as bait to expose Mr. Takekawa's evil deeds!

She was probably grouchy because she didn't have any energy to spare.

But now she just seemed sad and tired.

"You know, your punch really was impressive. And smartly delivered. I'm sure the girls who couldn't bring themselves to disclose that Mr. Takekawa had sexually harassed them are grateful to you, Tsumashina. They've got to be."

"……"

For just a second, Tsumashina seemed on the verge of tears, but she pressed her lips together tightly and held them in.

Still looking at the ground, she muttered, "I… I cried a lot, when I was a kid…so I wanted to get strong…"

There was no doubt in my mind that the vicious rumors were getting to Tsumashina.

"Well, I'd say you are very strong, and pretty cool, too," I told her.

"And you're quiet and nerdy," she replied.

"Yeah, well, tell me something I don't know…"

"What's your name…?"

"Huh?"

"I asked around for your name and which class you're in, but no one could remember. The only impression you left was of a plain boy in glasses."

She wants to know my name? Maybe so she can thank me?

"Musubu Enoki. I'm in your grade—first year, Class 1."

"...Oh, so you do have a name?"

"Of course I do! What, did you think my name was 'Plain Boy in Glasses'?"

A station worker approached us. "You two on your way to school?" he asked. We must have been making a bit of a scene on the train platform.

"Ah, she wasn't feeling well and needed to rest, but she's all right now, so we'll get going to school."

As if on cue, a train arrived.

"Come on, let's go."

I grabbed Tsumashina by the hand and pulled her on board.

"Sexual harassment..."

Inside the train carriage, Tsumashina glared at me with reproachful eyes, and I quickly let go.

"Ah, I didn't mean to! Sorry!"

I was freaking out about what would happen if I got nailed with one of her signature punches, but instead she let out a sigh of relief and grumbled, "...I guess it's all right."

She looks cute with a touch of red on her cheeks.

"Are you harassing someone? Musubu? I won't stand for it; I won't ever forgive, you know! I'll dance on your grave!"

I felt the chill of Princess Yonaga's hatred.

"Hang on, why did you suddenly go all pale?" Tsumashina asked. "Are you actually afraid of me?"

"No, I just get trainsick easily."

As I dodged the question, the train arrived at the stop closest to our school.

Of course, by the time we got there, the school gate had already closed.

We had to get tardy slips from the security guard, then go to the staff room and hand them to our homeroom teachers.

"Enoki, you go after me."

"Why?"

"I don't want them to think we were late together, do you? Then it would look like something was going on, wouldn't it? 'Cause there's absolutely not."

"Well, if there's nothing going on, we should be fine…"

"It definitely won't be fine."

We were bickering right in front of the gate, when—

"Ah! Hana!"

—some girls dressed in PE uniforms jogged toward us.

"Hana, I was worried! I sent you a text message, but you didn't read it. Thank goodness you're all right."

It seemed as though they were Tsumashina's classmates, but—

Wait…Hana?! Did she say Hana just now?

Isn't Tsumashina's first name Sanae?

Well, Pip did tell me that her Hana was a crybaby and that she worried because Hana got down easily.

But Tsumashina, a crybaby?

Though she did mention earlier that she cried a lot when she was little.

And she was sitting in the very station where Pip was left behind…

Hmm…

"By the way, Hana, what are you doing with Glasses Boy?"

"——"

"Hana's taken quite an interest in Mr. Glasses, hasn't she? She wanted to know his name and everything. Maybe—"

"W-we just happened to catch the same train!" Tsumashina frantically dismissed her friends' teasing.

Then I tactlessly asked my own questions.

"Tsumashina, when you were in elementary school, did you wear your hair in braids? And was your middle school uniform a blazer and pleated skirt with a red ribbon?"

"Huh…?"

This left Tsumashina and her friends flabbergasted.

"And was there a park in your neighborhood with a plesiosaur slide, and did you run away there once with a copy of Astrid Lindgren's *Pippi Longstocking*?"

"!"

Her face was the picture of shock.

Then, with her eyes wide-open, she contorted her lips to form words.

"How...could you possibly know...something like that...?" she whispered hoarsely.

My chest began to tremble, and it felt as though a sharp object had pierced straight through the center of my head. I was convinced.

Pip's owner, her Hana, is Tsumashina!

"Tsumashina, you lost something at that station a while ago, didn't you? Well, I found it! Your precious book!"

I finally found little Hana!

To think she was this close all along.

Her last name is probably different because of her parents' divorce, and I misread the characters in her first name—the characters that usually spell out "Sanae" can also be read as "Hana"!

Hana, who had been in her first year of middle school when they parted ways, now stood before me in her first year of high school.

With this revelation, I would be able to reunite Pip with Hana.

Ah, if I had known this would happen, I wouldn't have left her at home. I've got to go home right away and bring her back with me.

But as I turned to leave, Tsumashina's expression changed suddenly from bewilderment to dread, and she addressed me coldly.

"I don't know what you're talking about."

"Huh?"

"I never lost anything, and I don't know about that book. I don't want it."

Just as I thought I was going to be able to reunite Pip and Hana…

It was lunchtime.

I was slumped on the sofa in the music hall conference room while Haruto updated me on the results of his search for Hana.

"Her name was Hana Higuchi. When she was in her first year of middle school, her parents got divorced, and her mother got custody, so her family name changed to Tsumashina. The station where she left Pip behind was apparently close to where her father went to live with his new family after the divorce."

Pip had told me that, on the day she was lost, Hana had been sad all morning, and Pip had been concerned.

Hana had put her homemade cookies and the book she treasured like a friend into a paper bag, gotten off the train at an unfamiliar station, sat on a bench, and cried. She had definitely been planning to go see her father. But she must have had second thoughts after getting off the train.

Wouldn't she be burdening him by visiting his new family's home? Wouldn't she just be inconveniencing her father?

That was why she couldn't move from the bench. She couldn't bring herself to go out of the station gates and had instead gone back the way she'd come. Leaving the cookies and Pip behind on the bench in the bag she had been carrying…

"I think maybe she didn't forget the paper bag but actually left it there on purpose. Her father was the one who bought the book for her, and I can easily imagine wanting to let go of anything that reminded her of him."

Haruto's words made my heart sting.

So Hana didn't forget Pip—she abandoned her?

Then what's going to happen to her?

She loves Hana so much. All she wants is to be reunited.

I returned home from school still struggling to think of a way to break the news to Pip.

After setting Princess Yonaga down in the living room, I went up the stairs to the second floor and into my room.

Even Princess Yonaga, who would typically be accusing me of cheating right now, must have sensed the gravity of the situation. She didn't say a word.

"...I'm home, Pip."

"Welcome back, Musubu."

She seemed a little more worn out than before. Her voice was frail.

"You weren't bored here by yourself?"

"Oh, no. I just sat here thinking back on my time with Hana... When she was in her last year of elementary school, she went to Kyoto on a field trip. She was a real scaredy-cat, so she believed all the stories about ghosts in the old Kyoto inns, and the night before she went, she held me tight, shaking with fear. And then she crammed me into her backpack... We never saw any ghosts. Getting to go on trips with Hana...that was so much fun... And even though she was scared at first, once the field trip got underway, she smiled the whole time..."

She told her tale slowly...slowly, as if she were dreaming, then came to a stop.

"...Musubu, what's wrong? You're rubbing your eyes."

"J-just got some dust in them, that's all."

I promised her I would bring back some good news today.

I was sure I would know where to find Hana.

Pip didn't ask me anything more.

I'm sure she could guess that something was wrong just by looking at me, but she didn't cast blame or start grieving, just waited quietly for me to speak.

How can she be so kind?

Even though she had spent three years on public display in a train station hallway, she could still sympathize with other people. I'm sure she didn't feel as if she had been left there for that long.

"I'm sorry... Pip, I'm sorry I couldn't help you..."

I put my head down on the desk with a *thunk*.

I'm sorry.

I'm so sorry.

"Don't apologize... You're the one who heard my voice, Musubu. You came up to me and spoke back... There hadn't been anyone like you the whole time I was there...so I was really happy that you talked to me... Musubu, you're a really good person; you're so kind..."

But I wasn't able to grant Pip's wish.

I wasn't able to get her to see Hana.

Even though Hana was all she ever thought about.

"Musubu...I've got a request. Would you read me? I don't think your girlfriend will like it, but...just once? ...Please?"

It sounded as though she was making a final request.

She won't ever see Hana again.

I knew that was what she was thinking. Everything before my eyes became blurry. No matter how many times I blinked or rubbed with my fingers, I couldn't see clearly.

"Sure, I understand."

I sat down in my swivel chair, opened the cover with the picture of the girl in braids wearing tall socks, and started reading aloud.

"Way out at the end of a tiny little town was an old overgrown garden, and in the garden was an old house, and in the house lived Pippi Longstocking.

"She was nine years old, and she lived there all alone."

The series of easy words spelled out on the dry pages, all faded and yellowed, sank deep into my frayed heart.

This was Pip's story.

This was the Pip who had smiled so often at Hana the crybaby and scaredy-cat—the book that Hana had loved…

"She had no mother and no father, and that was of course very nice…

"…because there was no one to tell her to go to bed just when she was having the most fun."

With a suitcase full of gold coins and her monkey, Mr. Nilsson, in tow, the cheerful girl in tall socks moves into the Villa Villekulla. She is always looking for something fun to do. She is bold when she speaks, fearless, and the strongest girl in the world.

She does things like spread out a mountain of dough and plenty of flour on the floor to make heart-shaped ginger cookies; climb to the top of an oak tree carrying a teapot and cups to have a tea party; leap onto the circus stage to join the show and perform a splendid tightrope routine; and ride a raging bull.

"Hana cried at the drop of a hat, but whenever she read me, she would cheer up and start smiling just as quickly."

"Hana loved me, and I love-love-loved her back."

"I'm worried about her. On that day, she had been distracted all morning. She was so sad."

"I never want to see her like that again. I want to make her smile and laugh."

"I want to see Hana!"

It was that same strong, eager voice I had heard as I passed through the station gates. The voice of a lively young girl.

* * *

"Please take me to Hana."

"I've got to get back to Hana, no matter what."

On a lending shelf of a lonely train station, she had repeated her desperate, heart-wrenching plea.

"I want to see Hana. Someone please help me."

It had been three years since she had been left behind on a platform bench, in a bag with some ginger cookies, and yet…

"I wonder if Hana doesn't cry much anymore. Is she okay?"

"I bet I'll be able to see her soon. Hooray!"

The dry, yellow pages smelled sweet; there was a crumbly white dust falling out of the book where the spine and the pages were joined. I scanned the blurred words, rubbing my eyes all the while.

"Thank you, Musubu... But it's time for me to..."

As she thanked me in a fading voice, my own words caught in my throat.

"You can't!" I pleaded hoarsely. I pulled the volume adorned with a picture of the girl in braids toward me, entreating her with blurry red eyes—

"The person you want to read you isn't me, it's Hana, right? I swear I'll bring you back to her! So please hang on just a little longer!"

◇ ◇ ◇

The next day, I put Pip in my bag and left early for school.

After going to my classroom and leaving Pip in my desk, I headed for Tsumashina's classroom and waited for her in the hallway.

"Oh, Glasses Guy? You want to see Hana? Don't tell me you've fallen for her?"

One of her friends whom I had seen the day before in front of the school teased me, but I responded with a look of intense determination.

Perhaps because she saw how serious I was, she softened. "You know, Hana may be tough, but she cares about her friends and is a good person. She doesn't usually get violent at all, and it really bothered her that she wasn't able to thank you for helping her."

Before long, I glimpsed Tsumashina walking toward us with her school bag hanging off one shoulder. She seemed uneasy. I could feel the tension in my bones as I gave her a meaningful stare.

As soon as she noticed me, her expression hardened. She tried to ignore me and walk right past, so I grabbed her arm to stop her. Surprised, she immediately spun around and glared in contempt.

"What? I told you I don't know anything about that book. Let go."

"I can't do that."

I tightened my grip on Tsumashina's arm.

"Pip doesn't have much time left. After you forgot her at the station, she was put on the station lending shelf. All sorts of people read her, and she got worn out. Her cover and her pages are faded, and the glue in her spine is peeling. Despite all this, she's been worried about 'little Hana' the whole time. Hana was a crybaby, so she wants to make her smile again. She wants to see her friend again. All she wants is for her beloved Hana to read her one last time before she goes!"

Pip didn't know how much time had passed since she had parted from Hana. But she could feel her own body deteriorating day after day, and that was why she was calling out so desperately. She just wanted to see Hana one more time.

"Are you delusional? Books can't talk, dummy. What's your deal?"

I stared straight back at Tsumashina as she tried to shake her arm free, and I declared:

"I am—a voice for books!"

* * *

That's right! I alone can hear their voices! I can't ignore such fervent cries! I want to help them the best that I can!

Tsumashina widened her eyes, taken aback by my sudden ardor. But soon she scowled again.

"You're a creep after all. Let me go. If you don't—"

"You'll punch me in my face, too? Suit yourself. I don't care if you think I'm creepy. I know that I heard what Pip had to say, and I wanted to reunite her with 'little Hana,' so I searched everywhere for her. Pip was so happy when she told me about how Hana took her along to her middle school exams and on field trips, and about how much Hana loved her!"

Tsumashina's slender shoulders shook. She was probably confused as to how I could have known such personal details. I understood—after all, most people wouldn't believe someone who said he could hear the voices of books. But I wanted her to know how strongly Pip felt about her. I needed Tsumashina to know how badly Pip needed to see her.

She wanted it so intensely that she was begging everyone who passed her by, though her pleas went unheard.

On that day, I was the one who heard Pip's voice.

I was the one who heard her prayers.

And as her voice, I will convey her feelings to Tsumashina.

"Tsumashina, you claimed that you didn't forget anything at the station, that you don't know anything about a lost book, right? If that's true, then why did you get off at that station yesterday? You were sitting on that bench with a miserable look plastered on your face!"

"!"

Tsumashina drew her lips together tightly, as though barely holding back some great swell of emotion.

"At that station, three years ago—when you were in your first year of middle school—that's where you left Pip behind, together with some ginger cookies! You must remember that! That's why— That's why you got off at that station, isn't it? Pip told me that whenever you were feeling sad or having a tough time, you would read her to cheer up. Yesterday, weren't you distraught over the things people were saying about the incident with Mr. Takekawa? You wanted to read her, didn't you? So you returned to that place to remember those days with her, right? You regretted losing—"

"You're wrong!"

Tsumashina threw off my hand.

She looked at me with eyes like thunderclouds, darkened with all sorts of feelings—anger verging on tears, fear, disgust—and her lips shuddered as she spoke. "I didn't forget that book there. *I left it.*"

Her words pierced my chest and hollowed my soul.

The pain made me involuntarily place a hand over my own heart.

"Why did you do that? You loved Pip!"

"Because I stopped loving her."

Tsumashina's voice began to tremble and crack as she continued. "A little girl who lives a strange and wonderful life all by herself, who never has to go to school. She's got a suitcase full of gold coins and is strong enough to fight off any thieves. She's never heard of common sense or good manners. She's got no worries, even if her room is dirty or she breaks a plate or an adult gets mad at her, and she lives a carefree life doing as she pleases—that might have been a life I wanted as a kid, but once I grew up, I realized no girl could ever live like that, so I grew to hate her… I got sick and tired of that girl's adventures, didn't want to turn even one more page. So I threw her away."

She hadn't forgotten Pip—she had *discarded* her.

Those heartbreaking words landed with a thud.

There's no way I can let Pip hear this! She loves Hana too much! She'll fall to pieces from despair!

"If you've got that book, Enoki, you can throw it away. But don't speak to me about it ever again," Tsumashina demanded bluntly. She was guarded and tense.

With that, she went into her classroom.

Before I knew it, a huge crowd of people had gathered in the hallway, and all eyes were on me. But I had been so wounded by the exchange that I didn't even care.

"Word is going around that the boy with glasses, who provided testimony regarding the sexual harassment that resulted in Tsumashina sending Mr. Takekawa flying, approached her passionately and touched her against her will. Looks like you're famous now, Musubu. But no one knows your name; instead, they've been calling you 'Glasses Boy' or 'that plain guy' or 'the first-year.'"

It was lunchtime.

I had skipped first period and taken refuge in the music hall's conference room, where Haruto came to check in on me and deliver the news.

Ah, so in the end I'm only "the plain boy with glasses." Might as well just change my legal name at this point; that'd be just fine. Aaargh!

"...I can't face her."

I had begged her not to give up and sworn I would bring her to Hana. Now that I couldn't do that, it was impossible to bring myself to admit it, much less tell her that Hana had grown to hate her and had thrown her away on purpose.

I was certain that when I went back to the classroom and looked at Pip, the truth would be plain on my face. She was good at reading emotions, and I didn't want to disappoint her any more than I already had. That's why I had asked Haruto to let me escape to the music hall. I was nothing but a coward.

"I'd like to scribble *fool*, *incompetent*, and *idiot* on myself in ink a hundred times each..."

I sat on the sofa, groaning, with my head in my hands. I just wanted to writhe around on the floor. Though the floor of the conference room was covered in fluffy carpet, so it would probably end up feeling pretty good.

Haruto turned to me. "Well…I get the feeling you were too straightforward, which caused the opposite of what you intended, stirring up Tsumashina's emotions and making her angry."

"Uuugh."

"I don't think it was your fault." Haruto clapped a hand down gently on my shoulder. "I went and peeked into Tsumashina's classroom, and she was surrounded by friends. It looked like she was forcing herself to play it cool."

"Uuugh."

"As far as I can see, there's one last step."

One last step?

What does that mean?

In that moment, Haruto looked extremely dependable and grown-up as he said to me, "As thanks for your help with the Takekawa case, I can lend you my assistance one more step of the way."

◇ ◇ ◇

It was after school.

Tsumashina walked down the hall, staring at the floor. She probably had club activities to get to. She wore a T-shirt and track pants, and her bag hung from one shoulder.

She had chosen a route with little foot traffic, for as confidently as she behaved, she still didn't like people staring or whispering around her. In addition to the reputation she had gained as the ferocious girl who had dealt a mean right cross to a predatory teacher, she was now saddled with rumors about her getting an early-morning love confession from an unassuming first-year with glasses. No doubt she was fed up with it all.

"Tsumashina?"

When she heard someone call her name, she looked up defensively. But her expression changed quickly to one of confusion.

The person speaking to Tsumashina was someone everyone in school knew, the son of the chair of the school board, the third-year student who conducted the orchestra club—Haruto Himekura.

He was tall enough to be a model and was gorgeous yet somehow approachable. He had a certain grace about him, even just standing there. Tsumashina must have been shocked to have a VIP suddenly speak to her, and as you would expect, there was no way she could glare at the Campus Prince with open hostility.

"Wh-what is it...?"

Tsumashina's shrill tone of voice betrayed her nervousness.

Haruto spoke in a gentlemanly tone. "The first-year Musubu Enoki, you know him, right?"

"!" Tsumashina's cheek twitched.

"Actually, I've been entrusted by Musubu with a book."

Tsumashina's shoulders shook slightly.

Upon hearing my name, and that he was carrying a book for me, she must have known exactly what title it was.

Haruto extended the manila envelope he was holding.

I won't take it—before Tsumashina could say something like that, Haruto interrupted.

"I wonder if you could return it to Musubu for me."

"Huh?"

She was obviously struggling to decide how to answer such an unusual request from someone so unexpected.

"I'm counting on you."

Haruto handed over the manila envelope and gracefully took his leave.

Only someone like Haruto had the subtlety to make a request without actually asking anything.

"...Why me?" Tsumashina mumbled. She looked down at the envelope, distraught.

There was no way she could just toss aside a package entrusted to her by the Campus Prince.

"...Enoki might still be in his classroom."

She was probably planning to hand it over quickly and be done with it. She started to turn back toward the first-year classrooms—and her feet came to a quick stop right in the middle of the hallway.

"......"

The weight of the object in her hand felt awfully familiar…
Hesitating, she stared down at the paper envelope.

"Hana?"

Tsumashina could not hear the cheerful voice calling out to her through the thin paper of the manila envelope.

"Hana, Hana!"

She stood there motionless, staring at the envelope, almost as if she had somehow noticed the voice she couldn't possibly have heard.

The mouth of the brown envelope was folded over just slightly. It wasn't sealed. She held her breath and rested her fingers on the fold.

With a rustle of paper, she lifted up the flap. Her fingers stopped, as if startled by the sensation.

She stared down at the envelope again and let out a sigh—then nervously grasped the opening once more.

Her face distorted into a painful grimace, as though she were fighting against something inside herself, and she ground her teeth. As if she were doing something untoward, she glanced behind her. At a loss, she stood frozen to the ground.

"Hana."

She frowned, opened the nearest door—which happened to lead to the biology room—and went inside.

"Hana, Hana!"

Packed with beakers and specimen jars, the biology room was darkened by blackout curtains hanging over the windows. She impatiently turned on a lamp, set her bag down on one of the black heat-resistant tables, and stood beside it as she opened the manila envelope and looked inside.

It held a children's book, one size larger than a standard paperback.

Just by looking at the yellowed pages, she could tell it was the precious book she brought everywhere in childhood.

The moment she put her hand in the envelope and touched the cover, both Pip and Tsumashina must have shuddered.

Looking at the girl in braids with a monkey on her arm, who was wearing tall socks that came up above her knees and big shoes that were floppy in front, Tsumashina frowned again. Her eyes began to fill with tears.

"Hana, I finally found you!"

A voice called out to Tsumashina, bursting with excitement.

"I found you again. I'm happy, Hana. So happy!"

Tsumashina opened the thoroughly worn-out and faded cover. With trembling fingers, she began reading timidly.

"Way out at the end of a tiny little town was an old overgrown garden, and in the garden was an old house, and in the house lived Pippi Longstocking."

There was no doubt about it—she still remembered the story. She had read that nostalgic opening paragraph over and over and over and over again since she was small.

The words slipped warmly, gently into her turbulent mind, and she could no longer stop herself.

Like a thirsty traveler searching for water who finally arrives at an oasis, scoops up cold water with both hands and pours it down their throat, sprinkles it over their face, then finally submerges their whole body in the water, she kept turning the pages as if in a trance.

"Pippi was indeed a remarkable child. The most remarkable thing about her was that she was so strong.

* * *

"She was so very strong that in the whole wide world there was not a single police officer as strong as she."

It's the tale of a girl with braided pigtails wearing long socks up over her knees and big floppy shoes, who grabs her monkey—Mr. Nilsson—and a suitcase full of gold coins one day and moves into the weed-covered Villa Villekulla.

Tommy and Annika, the siblings who live next door, soon become good friends with Pippi. Together, they become "*Thing*-Finders," have tea parties at the top of a tree, go on kids-only excursions, and have fun playing together.

"The whole world is full of things, and somebody has to look for them. And that's just what a Thing-Finder does."

Tsumashina had said she came to hate Pippi after she grew up.

"A little girl who lives a strange and wonderful life all by herself, who never has to go to school. She's got a suitcase full of gold coins and is strong enough to fight off any thieves. She's never heard of common sense or good manners. She's got no worries, even if her room is dirty or she breaks a plate or an adult gets mad at her, and she lives a carefree life doing as she pleases—that might have been a life I wanted as a kid, but once I grew up, I realized no girl could ever live like that, so I grew to hate her... I got sick and tired of that girl's adventures, didn't want to turn even one more page. So I threw her away."

In Pippi's house, there is no father or mother to call her own. But the book frames that as desirable. After all, there is no one to tell her it's time for bed when she is in the middle of playing. When she was a child, Tsumashina had probably envied that about Pippi.

But once her parents divorced and her father left, she could no longer see that as a "good thing." Suddenly, it was painful to look at Pippi, the strong-willed girl who lives alone and is just fine even if she doesn't go to school.

* * *

"This book is full of lies!"

"How can she be okay without a father or mother?"

"Why does Pippi always have the energy to do as she pleases? Her life is nothing but fun! While I'm in terrible pain every day."

That's what Tsumashina had probably thought—

But she's grown up a lot since then. She must realize Pippi's story also includes loneliness and isolation; Pippi isn't just a girl who is happy all the time. Now that she's older, Tsumashina must be able to read between the lines to see what is hidden within the cheerful, happy-go-lucky tale.

"'Have I behaved badly?'

"'Goodness, I didn't know that.'

"...she added and looked very sad."

The first time Pippi ever attends school, she is disruptive and then is promptly abandoned by her teacher, who tells her she never needs to come to school again.

She is overjoyed to be invited over to Tommy and Annika's house and tries her best to dress up to go out. But the lady of the house frowns on her because she doesn't follow social etiquette, and she tells her that someone with manners as poor as hers isn't welcome.

"Pippi looked at her in astonishment and her eyes slowly filled with tears. 'That's just what I was afraid of,' she said. 'That I couldn't behave properly. It's no use to try; I'll never learn. I should have stayed on the ocean'...

"...And Pippi ran up to her and whispered, 'Forgive me because I couldn't behave myself. Good-bye!'"

* * *

On both occasions, Pippi immediately acts as if nothing had happened and seems to go right back to her usual cheerful, daring self. She never reconciles with the adults later on. She doesn't go back to school, and her manners remain poor.

She lives a strong life on her own.

She is a truly special girl.

And yet, Pippi has a kind of sadness about her.

She has a certain loneliness.

Tsumashina didn't realize it when she was a child, but now that she has more perspective, she ought to appreciate Pippi even more, I think.

"Don't you worry about me. I'll always come out on top."

And then, immersing herself in the adventures of a girl with freckles and braids who casts off her sadness and smiles a dazzling smile—the story of the strongest girl in the world—brings back that forgotten childhood thrill, and she can't help but smile.

"—When Hana read me, she stopped crying and even smiled and giggled."

Surely Tsumashina must realize it herself.

Tears are streaming down her face, yet she's still smiling happily.

Seeing her upset, Pip continued to cheerfully encourage her.

"I love you, Hana."

"I'm so happy to have you read me again."

"You've grown a lot, Hana."

"You're still crying, but you're smiling, too, so I'm sure you're all right."

* * *

"Hana, I love you! Hana, Hana, I love you, I love you! I love you."

With every turn of the page, she kept repeating the words *I'm happy, I love you*, and *I'm happy* like bright bursts of light.

"I'm happy."

"I'm so happy."

Clear drops of liquid ran down Tsumashina's cheeks, dripping onto the yellowed pages. Pip's voice quivered. **"I love you,"** she repeated again.

As Tsumashina turned a page, it came loose from the book's spine and fell gently onto her knee.

"!"

She gasped as page after page after page came loose and fell from her hands.

"W-wait, why?!"

Eyes full of tears, Tsumashina struggled to hold on to the pages, all while Pip continued to comfort her even as she fell to pieces.

"I love you, Hana. I love you!"

As a lending book, Pip had been read by a great number of people and was sometimes handled roughly. Her life span as a book had long since reached its limit, and she had held out only because of her fervent desire to see Hana once more.

Now that Hana's hands turned her pages, her wish had come true. Her body trembled with happiness, even as her life came to an end.

"No! Why, oh no!"

Tsumashina gathered up the fallen pages, crying the whole time.

"Thank you for reading me again, Hana. I'll always love you!"

Pip's final words rang full of gratitude. Then, nothing.

Only Tsumashina's tear-choked voice echoed through the silent biology room as she bent over the floor, grasping at the pages.

"No, no, no…you can't go."

I had been peeking in the whole time from the hallway, and this was enough to make me blink and start sniffling, then flop down on the floor and burst into tears.

Pip, I'm so glad you were able to get Hana to read you in the end.

I'm glad we made it in time.

I'm sure you were the happiest a book could be as you went.

I was sure of it, yet I still couldn't stop crying.

It didn't take long for Tsumashina to discover me, as she could hear the sound of my snuffling from where I was peeking in at her from the hall.

"I can't believe you got Himekura involved in all this. And what do you have to cry about, Enoki?"

Even as she poured on the complaints, Tsumashina couldn't seem to stop crying, either. For a while, the two of us stood there with tears streaming down our faces.

"At the end, Pip thanked you for reading her again and said she'll always love you, Hana."

Tsumashina listened without anger, and her scowl had faded. "…I still don't believe you can hear the voices of books or whatever… But if Pip really did say that, then I'm glad. I always regretted leaving her behind… So I'm happy I was able to read her one last time…"

Tsumashina embraced the manila envelope that held the loose pages and bowed deeply to me. "While I was reading, I really felt deep love for her. The book who loved me so much may have fallen to pieces, but I'll keep her pages as a precious memento. And I'll buy a copy of her next adventure to read."

Tsumashina looked adorably sheepish as she mumbled with a grin, "I hope the new book comes to love me, too…"

She smiled up at me, and I could see her cheeks were a little red. She looked to the side, flustered.

And then, as we parted, she reassured with determination:

* * *

"Don't you worry about me. I'll always come out on top."

It was a line from *Pippi Longstocking.*

Tsumashina blushed slightly again, then turned bashfully around and broke into a run. I watched her go, feeling invigorated.

Pip, it looks like Hana will be okay after all.

Well, I'd better get home and try to placate Princess Yonaga. I made her stay home alone again, so I bet she's so upset, she won't talk for a while. Though I'm sure winning her over will be amusing enough—I walked off with light steps.

Book 2

An Urgent Request from *Steam from Another World ☆ The Great Giggling Battle*

For as long as I can remember, I have somehow been able to hear the voices of books. Library books have quiet voices and speak in whispers.

The books in secondhand stores are relaxed and cheerful, as if they're talking over tea.

And the books stacked up in the new-releases section of the major bookstore in the station building are overflowing with energy, chattering like recently hatched chicks.

"Read me! I'm very interesting!"

"Come and read me! You won't regret it!"

"If you read me, you'll be moved to tears!"

They all simultaneously make their claims.

"Read me!"

"Buy me!"

"Read me!"

"Be my first reader!"

Standing in front of the lively new-publications section was a pale figure of a man, looking like a spirit that had just emerged from a graveyard.

Huh? That guy was here yesterday, too, wasn't he?

He was still young and appeared to be in his mid to late twenties. But since he was here in a bookstore in the early afternoon, wearing a sloppy shirt and pants, he couldn't have been a salaryman. With lanky limbs and a thin body, he seemed as if he could have been blown away by a stiff breeze. His expression was timid and apprehensive, darkened by nerves and restlessness.

When I first saw him the day before, I had wondered if he was there to shoplift, but he didn't seem to have the disposition or the physical strength to do anything bad. Instead, he seemed to be putting all his effort into drawing his body in smaller, as if physically apologizing for his existence.

The books were ardently addressing this man, and I could hear chattering from a pile of light novels that had just gone on sale yesterday.

"Mayu Mayu, are you all right? Did you eat a proper meal today?"

"Cheer up, Mayu Mayu! I'm sure someone will buy us."

"You can do it, Mayu Mayu! We'll do our best to get bought!"

A chorus of voices that sounded as though they belonged to girls in an anime cheered for "Mayu Mayu."

On the other hand—

"Please buy us!"

"We'll make your heart pound and give you a thrill!"

"Come on, make me yours!"

—they were hawking themselves, mostly to male customers, like indie pop idols trying to sell CDs at a merch table.

They had also sparked my curiosity yesterday, but Princess Yonaga had rebuked me from inside my bag: "Musubu, let's go home at once. You've got me, so you don't need any more books, do you? I've cursed your eyes to rot in their sockets if you stare at the cover of another book for more than three seconds. If we don't leave this store immediately, your eyes will start to decay into mush, and then you'll never be able to read me again."

I hadn't lingered.

But today, Princess Yonaga was back home in my room.

"You're planning on cheating on me, aren't you? Not on my watch!"

She had been upset about it.

I tried to put her in a good mood, bringing my face so close to the indigo cover that the frame of my glasses nearly touched it, then whispering to her that that wasn't true, that she was the only girlfriend for me, but she just pouted.

"Don't even try. I'm cursing you!"

Anyway, I couldn't help but be curious when I encountered the same customer who had caught my eye the day before, in the same place for a second time.

Today, as yesterday, I could hear female voices encouraging him from the pile of newly published light novels.

"Mayu Mayu, yesterday someone took one of us home!"

"We're doing our very best to call out to the customers so that they pick more of us up!"

"Oh gentlemeeen! We'll show you all our most embarrassing parts! Take us home and enjoy us at your leisure!"

When I peeked over in the direction of the voices, I saw a pile of books with a picture of girls soaking in a hot spring on the cover.

All the girls had towels wrapped around them, but they were exposing most of their chests and barely keeping their breasts hidden, or they were sitting on rocks with their plump thighs crossed one over the other or were sticking their legs up out of the hot spring water. Sexy poses all around.

One of the girls was blonde and had an air of nobility; one looked like a gallant lady knight; and one looked like a soothing older-sister type with a nice body and ears that tapered to a point, along with a devilish tail growing from her backside. Another girl had cat ears and a flat chest and wore a blank expression. Last was a girl with glasses, soaking in the hot spring while wearing a large tricornered hat on her head.

The title of the book was a total cliché: *Steam from Another World ☆ The Great Giggling Battle—How a NEET like Me Reincarnated in Another World, Used My New Superpowers to Excavate a Hot Spring, and Formed a Harem!*

It caught my interest, since it was a genre I didn't usually read, and when I went to take a look, the books suddenly made a commotion.

"He's looking!"

"He's looking at us with paaassion!"

"A student? Middle school? High school? We're not R-rated, so you can use your allowance to buy us!"

"Take me home with you! I'll really make your heart pound!"

They tried to sell themselves.

Aside from the girls, I felt the clammy sensation of someone's eyes on me. Turning to the side to look, I locked eyes with the lanky man they had all been calling "Mayu Mayu."

He looked surprised and quickly averted his eyes. But perhaps my presence made him uneasy, because he kept glancing at me out of the corner of his eye.

"It's all right, Mayu Mayu. I'm sure that Glasses Boy is going to buy us!"

"That's right, Mayu Mayu. He's been staring at us hungrily."

Hungrily? I don't remember looking at you that way.

At this point, I realized something important. The author's name, written right below the title, was Mayu Sasaki.

Mayu? Mayu Mayu? Aha!

"By any chance, would you be Mayu Sasaki?"

When I asked this of the fidgety man beside me, he leaped into the air as if he were in some kind of comedy sketch, went deathly pale, and stammered, "H-h-how do you know that I'm Mayu Sasaki?"

He loudly blurted out his question, then clapped both hands over his mouth. Then his shoulders drooped, and he began slowly rocking back and forth. "I… I said it. From my own mouth."

Ah, maybe that was the wrong move.

"I'm sorry; it's just that I happened to see you here yesterday, too, so I wondered if you might be the author."

"Ha-ha…ha-ha-ha-ha… It's unseemly, isn't it? Loitering around the new-releases section because I'm worried about sales. I'm sure people would be put off if they knew that the author who goes by the cute pen name Mayu Sasaki, also known as Mayu Mayu, was actually a shabby old man… Hnnnnngggg, you've got to keep this a secret!"

Mayu Mayu bowed repeatedly. "My real name is Asatomu Sasaki, but I thought using a lady's name would draw in more male readers and increase sales. I even planned ahead and made up the adorable nickname Mayu Mayu. But the writing style and story were obviously from an old man, and now I've been found out. A guy like me trying to channel a sixteen-year-old high school girl is just cringey. Please don't post about this on social media or anything."

"Mayu Mayu, you're exposing your own secrets again."

"You told him all about your ploy."

Mayu Mayu was getting light-headed from bowing so much and was starting to stagger. I assured him that I wouldn't be posting on social media and that I wouldn't tell anyone.

"R-really? Thank you, thank you. In that case, um…if you like, um… well…"

He must have a very reserved personality.

He didn't seem to be able to work up the courage to ask me to buy a copy, and he simply stood there fidgeting while red in the face. In his place, the books Mayu Mayu had penned called out to me.

"Buy us!"

"Buy us!"

"Well then…since I came all this way."

When I picked up a copy from the pile of books, his face lit up like the sun.

"Thank you! Ah! I'll sign it for you. What's your name?"

"Musubu Enoki. Um, I haven't bought it yet, so…"

"Wah! You're right. Okay then, I'll sign after you pay. Yeah, I brought my signing pen and everything."

"…Uh-huh."

If I take home a signed book, Princess Yonaga is going to blow up. Not to mention that there are five half-naked girls in alluring poses on the cover.

"Cheating on me...shall not be tolerated. Not ever."

Her cold voice played in my head as a shiver shot down my spine.

But I couldn't exactly break it to Mayu Mayu that I wouldn't be able to buy his book or that I didn't want his signature just because of how *she* would react, especially when he was so overjoyed.

* * *

Ten minutes later—

With my copy of *Steam from Another World ☆ The Great Giggling Battle—How a NEET like Me Reincarnated in Another World, Used My New Superpowers to Excavate a Hot Spring, and Formed a Harem!* in hand, complete with a message and signature written on the inside of the cover in pink pen reading *To Musubu Enoki, from Mayu Mayu*, I sat drinking tea in the dining section of the nearest convenience store with the author himself.

"Sorry I couldn't take you to the pancake place with the long line. I don't get my royalties on the book for two more months, so finances are a little tight. I've been living off bean sprouts all week."

"You know, I can pay."

I set the hundred yen for his iced coffee on the table, but he pushed it right back at me. "No, no, no! I can't let a fan pay for more than the book!" he asserted passionately.

Since when am I a "fan"...?

"Besides, this was the first time I've seen someone buy my book with my own eyes since I started my career as an author seven years ago. To think that it would bring me such joy!"

"Seven years? You've been doing this for that long?"

"...My books don't sell at all, but I publish one every year."

Mayu Mayu's shoulders dropped heavily again.

The book he had made out to me and signed said encouragingly, "**Chin up, Mayu Mayu. If the books sell, you can put out a sequel, and you'll have income and stability once they get turned into a series. Then you can eat until you're full!**"

He sounded gloomy. "I've been thinking of this book as my last chance. When I was a student, I won lots of prizes for my writing, so I kept right on doing it and didn't look for another job. But I think I've reached my limit. I've mostly given up at this point."

"Oh no."

"Aaaaaah, but I packed this book with foreshadowing and stuff pointing to a sequel, even though I don't know whether there will be one or not! Hnnnngggg, I'm such a dummy! *Of course* they're going to ax it after the first volume, right? I pulled my readers into another canceled series, urgh. Hang on, do I even have any readers? Do I? Readers?"

"Th-there's me," I offered, despite my better judgement. "I'll read it. Since I'm a fan."

Mayu Mayu took my hand in both of his and squeezed firmly, then pumped it up and down several times.

"Thank you, thank you, thank you......"

"Musubu, thank you. I'll take good care of you!"

Getting thanked by both the author and the book at the same time was a very rare experience, so I was glad to help. But I knew I would have to keep Princess Yonaga from finding out.

"...You smell like another woman."

Eep!

As soon as I stepped into my room back home, I heard a cold voice from atop my bed.

Spread out beside my pillow was a lace handkerchief. On it, a book with an indigo cover lay in wait—my unfathomably jealous girlfriend, Princess Yonaga, emanating an icy aura from the thin body of her book.

Inside the school backpack hanging from my shoulders was a brand-new, signed copy of another book, addressed in my name.

All along the way home, I had impressed upon the book that no matter what happened, she must not say a word, that it was in her best interest to keep quiet.

"Musubu, you can talk to us, huh? I'm still new to this world, but you're the first person like that I've met."

Steamy (that's what I had decided to call the book) was surprised by this, but she seemed to have an obedient nature and swore that she understood, that she wouldn't talk at all, that she would be silent.

Despite those reassurances, the second I entered my room, Princess Yonaga sniffed her out.

Should I play dumb or get down and beg forgiveness…?

"Huh? What are you talking about? Don't be silly. There's no way I would be distracted by other books when I have you, Princess Yonaga."

Of course, I couldn't tell her that not only had I been distracted but I had even gotten my name written in the book. All I could do was feign innocence.

"…Musubu, you sound even more insincere than usual when you lie."

I jumped in fright again. Starting to sweat, I answered as sincerely as I could muster.

"Is that so? I don't think that's true."

"And your nose twitches."

"Huh?!" I covered my nose in a panic.

"Your eyeballs dart around, and you sigh before you speak, and you tilt your head a little to the side, and you try hard to look sweet."

"Huh? Huh?"

Am I really that easy to read? Or are Princess Yonaga's powers of observation on another level? Come to think of it, tilting your head and smiling sweetly before telling a lie is something a con man would do.

"There's another woman in your bag… She smells of the bath salts at a hot spring…"

"B-bath salts, huh—? Princess Yonaga, you've never taken a bath, have you?"

"It's similar to how you smell when you get out of the bath…"

"That's because the bath salts we use at home are from a line put out by a famous hot spring."

"Did you get in the bath with a book who's not me? Did you give her a little peep show?"

"What are you talking about?!"

Welp, guess my cover's blown.

"Cheaters…will not be tolerated… I'll curse you… I'll dance on your grave!"

Ah, now she's entered "darkness mode."

"I curse, curse you! Musubu, tomorrow when you wake up, this land shall be transformed into a hell of rampant pestilence... And all because you were unfaithful!"

"I wasn't! I wasn't unfaithful, really! Ah, I think it's almost time for dinner, so I'm going downstairs, okay? See you later."

I said this with a smile, then descended the stairs while carrying my backpack.

In the living room, I let out a sigh and gently unzipped my bag.

"Sorry, that was probably pretty scary. But she won't bite. I think."

I spoke to Steamy, who was huddled in the bottom of my bag.

"Musubu, your girlfriend really is the controlling type, huh...? That's gotta be rough. I feel for you..."

She sympathized with me. But that wasn't all. **"I'll heal your pain for you, Musubu. Come on, today you can read me to your heart's content."**

Ah geez, she's so nice... Who wouldn't feel their heart skip a beat at such an innocent suggestion?

By no means was I suddenly ready to give my heart to a new girl. Yet, that evening, I read through Mayu Mayu's newest publication in the safety of my big sister's vacant room—she was off studying at a university in Hokkaido.

The main character in the book, a NEET and a recluse, slips and dies in a bathhouse, then is reincarnated in another world, where he excavates a hot spring and becomes a hero who is popular with the ladies. The story follows the title exactly, and it was a fun and easy read.

"Whoa, this book has great pacing."

"Doesn't it? Doesn't it? Mayu Mayu always stresses so hard over choosing the right words so that he can tell his story in short sentences. That way, people who aren't great at reading and people who are tired from the day can read his books comfortably."

"The plot developments come quickly, and even as I'm reading the story,

I'm anxious to find out what's coming next. I really want to see the main character mow down some bad guys!"

"That's coming up soon! And after that, it's time for him to enjoy being with the princess!"

"Princess Elaina is so graceful and innocent and lovely!"

"My favorite character, the cat girl Tiara, is so standoffish at first, but she softens up and even sits on his lap and lets him pamper her, and it's suuuuuuper cute! I highly recommend that part."

"Huh, seriously? I want to read that right away!"

"Sure, read on, read on!"

It was fun to pass time chatting with Steamy as I turned the pages. All the girls in the story were cute, and I was impressed by the way the book established different tastes, preferences, and backgrounds for each of them. The love with which the author had carefully written each character really shone through, making me feel all warm and fuzzy. I felt I now understood why Mayu Mayu had been so concerned about his books.

"Wow! That was great!"

Having finished reading it in one go, I stretched both arms out while still sitting cross-legged on the floor. I felt energized. Even my body felt lighter.

"Wasn't it?! Mayu Mayu's books are the best in the world!"

"I definitely want to read the sequel! There was a lot of foreshadowing in there."

"I'm sure lots of copies of this book will sell, and he'll write many more!"

We both discussed how much we were looking forward to it, and it was really fun speculating with Steamy about future plot developments.

When I returned to my own room to sleep, Princess Yonaga greeted me with a frigid remark. "**...Musubu, you stabbed me in the back...you filthy cheater!**"

At least, that's what she said, but...

I wasn't cheating. It's okay to read other books sometimes...

The next day after school, I went to the same bookstore inside the train station, together with Steamy, who was in my bag.

I wanted to give Mayu Mayu my impressions and let him know that I had a lot of fun reading his book and that I was looking forward to reading the next part of the story. I figured he would probably be there again, fretting over his sales.

As expected, Mayu Mayu was in front of the same table in the new-releases section. But while he had been fidgety and restless yesterday, today he stood there bearing an expression of full-on despair. He seemed as if he was about to go jump off the train platform or dive from a high building.

"What's wrong?"

"M-my books are—"

Now that he mentioned it, I realized I couldn't hear any voices cheering Mayu Mayu on. When I glanced down at the table, I realized the entire display was different—his books had been replaced.

The space had been filled with a long-awaited new release in the *Hard-Boiled High Schooler: Suzuhito Narihira* series by popular author Kaito Suzunomiya. Wraparound ad sleeves adorning the books proclaimed that both volumes would release at once, and the table was buried under a staggering number of copies.

The *Suzuhito Narihira* series was quite popular, having already been adapted into dramas and anime series several times, as well as a movie. Apparently, this was an especially noteworthy release, since the first new book in two years was going on sale in conjunction with the airing of a drama adaptation, so the bookstore must have stocked up in anticipation of record sales. It looked as though they had taken down the other new releases to make space.

"I'm certain there's just one copy of my book left as a placeholder on the shelf, and the rest have been returned… Aaaaagh, it's only the third day since the on-sale date, but of all things, I had to compete with the newest release of the *Suzuhito Narihira* series? And to top it all off, a simultaneous release of a two-parter? Young readers only have so much pocket money to spend, and no one's going to have anything left over to buy my book after they buy two volumes of *Suzuhito Narihira*!"

The *Suzuhito Narihira* books were flying off the shelves even as Mayu

Mayu threw a fit. Some people were buying two copies each of the first and second books, and a few were even grabbing three of each. Cool and confident voices echoed from the stacked-up books.

"Yeah...you've been waiting for me!"

"Come on, I'll let you read me! I'll make you restless with intrigue!"

"Hey now, if you don't hurry up and buy me, I'll sell out and you'll be in tears!"

Beside the shelf, a pale Mayu Mayu grumbled to himself.

"I'm finished. Another cancellation. And it was my first new book in a year, the one the editing council had been waiting six months for… They won't publish my next one, since they never go anywhere…"

"Don't say that—other bookstores probably have your books on display for sale, don't you think? And besides, people can order online."

"That's right, Mayu Mayu. Cheer up!"

Steamy and I both tried to encourage him, but Mayu Mayu was drowning in negativity.

"Did you know? When you enter a title into the search bar of an online bookshop, it displays the sales rankings in real time. When I looked earlier, the new *Suzuhito Narihira* volumes held first and second place, and my *Steam from Another World ☆ The Great Giggling Battle—How a NEET like Me Reincarnated in Another World, Used My New Superpowers to Excavate a Hot Spring, and Formed a Harem!* was ranked one thousand three hundred fifty-secooond!"

One thousand three hundred fifty-second place? That is harsh…

"To top it all off, its single precious review is a one-star rating that says, 'The writing is choppy, and there are too many paragraph breaks. The plot is lascivious wish-fulfillment garbage. The cookie-cutter heroines are boring. It's in bad faith for the author to include so much foreshadowing when we don't even know if there will be any future volumes. The one star is for the illustrations.' Waaah!"

"How cruel! That person must have hardly read it! All of Mayu Mayu's novels are fantastic—we're very, very interesting!"

I found myself agreeing with the book wholeheartedly.

"I read your newest book yesterday, and it was really, really fun!" I insisted. "The heroines were all so adorable and attractive that my girlfriend accused me of cheating! I couldn't put it down, and I read the whole thing before I realized it!"

I put real effort into my review, but Mayu Mayu's shoulders still drooped.

"It's fine, really… I had a feeling things might turn out this way… Why did I bother with so much foreshadowing…even though it was clear as day that there wasn't going to be another volume? Aaaugh…I'm sorry, I'm sorry for the foreshadowing…!"

Completely overcome by anguish, Mayu Mayu seemed as if he was going to crouch down on the spot despite the fact that he was in public.

To be fair, making a comeback at this point would likely be difficult.

But I want to see how the story continues and get to know more about its charming heroines! I don't want him to give up in the face of one stupid, nasty review!

That's right: I'm a voice for books—and I want everyone to read this light, refreshing story.

Just as he had gripped my hands the day before, I took both of Mayu Mayu's hands in mine and squeezed them. "If your book sells, you'll be able to put out a sequel, right? In that case, let's sell them! It's not over yet! Let's do everything we can!"

At lunch the following day, there was an unusual commotion in the cafeteria of Seijou Academy.

The son of the school's chairwoman, third-year student Haruto Himekura, who served as the director of the orchestra club as per family tradition and was nicknamed the Campus Prince, unexpectedly graced the cafeteria and sat on the terrace.

"Huh? No way! Haruto's here?"

"This is the first time I've ever seen him in the cafeteria. Doesn't he usually get expensive meals delivered and eat them in his private room in the music hall?"

It went without saying that he attracted a lot of attention because of his family, but with looks like his, he would have stood out even if nobody knew his name. The star student on campus proceeded to buy coffee from the vending machine. That somehow won him even more attention.

"Whoa, Himekura drinks vending machine coffee?"

"I thought he was a tea person. I heard he likes Darjeeling."

"He's so cool! Just watching him on the terrace drinking coffee, it's like I can see the scenery of Paris stretching out behind him."

When Haruto took a paperback from his jacket pocket and held it up in such a way that the cover was clearly visible, even more sounds of surprise reverberated throughout the room.

"!"

"!"

"!"

On the shocking cover, with an anime-style illustration that included a cat girl, a demon lady, and a blonde princess soaking in a hot spring bath with towels wrapped seductively around their bodies, was printed an even more unbelievable title: *Steam from Another World ☆ The Great Giggling Battle—How a NEET like Me Reincarnated in Another World, Used My New Superpowers to Excavate a Hot Spring, and Formed a Harem!*

"A harem?"

"*The Great Giggling Battle*?"

"Reincarnated in another world…? Superpowers…? A hot spring…?"

The bustling cafeteria fell silent, and whispers rippled through the students like waves.

"Haruto is reading a light novel!"

"And it's the cutesy fantasy type?!"

Students went running from the cafeteria, spreading the news. Everyone wondered what on earth had gotten into the pedigreed prince of the school.

"It's terrible! Haruto is reading something called *The Great Giggling Battle* in the cafeteria! It's an *isekai* story!"

The news spread online, too, with pictures to boot, and then other students who had heard about it that way surged into the cafeteria and made a huge commotion.

"He's really reading a light novel!"

"It's *The Great Giggling Battle*!"

"A steamy hot spring harem!"

Haruto pretended as if he didn't hear the uproar going on around him and gracefully turned a page.

Steamy was utterly ecstatic to have her pages turned so gently by his long fingers. **"This guy's way of reading is so gentlemanly and amazing… Plus, everyone is looking this way. I'm getting tingles having my pages turned while so many people are watching!"** she mumbled.

The day before, after declaring to Mayu Mayu that there was still something we could do, I had returned to school and waited for the orchestra club to finish practicing so I could approach Haruto with a proposal.

"Haruto, I have a request! Please read this book somewhere where as many people as possible will see you!"

He had stared at the long title and the cover with the girls bathing in their tiny towels without the slightest change in expression.

"Musubu, you know there's no way I can turn you down when you make a request with that earnest face of yours, but this time you're really going to owe me."

I nodded to myself.

I'm just not going to think about what he's going to want in return.

The voices of the students swarmed around me.

"I wonder if that light novel is really all that interesting? Maybe I should try reading it, too."

"I ordered it online a second ago."

"I've got to swing by the bookstore on the way home."

"I'll buy it, too!"

And—

* * *

"Incredible… I've imagined it so many times, but to see my own book selling right before my eyes…"

After school. The bookstore in the station.

Students in Seijou Academy uniforms flooded the area around the new-release section.

"Which one is *The Great Giggling Battle*?"

"The one over there with the hot spring on the cover."

"Excuse me, but I'm looking for the new release from Mayu Sasaki?"

They were all hunting for Mayu Mayu's book and heading to the register with copies in hand.

The one copy that had been stuck on a shelf was immediately snatched up, and after that, so many people must have been inquiring where they could find *The Great Giggling Battle* that soon all the copies of *Steam from Another World ☆ The Great Giggling Battle—How a NEET like Me Reincarnated in Another World, Used My New Superpowers to Excavate a Hot Spring, and Formed a Harem!* had been returned to the new-releases display.

The pile of books disappeared in the blink of an eye.

Sitting beside them, the books from the *Suzuhito Narihira* series remarked:

"Oh, what's this? You girls are really mounting some good competition against us!"

"I'll be sure to remember your title!"

All of Steamy's sister books shouted words of gratitude:

"Thank you for buying me!"

"I'm so happy! Thank you!"

"I love you! Thank you!"

They also showered Mayu Mayu with praise:

"Mayu Mayu, you did it!"

"You can put out a sequel, Mayu Mayu!"

As for the author himself, he was in a tizzy. "Is this a dream? Did I die suddenly in my sleep and get reincarnated in another world?"

From that point, *The Great Giggling Battle* continued to sell, and when all the copies at the bookstore in the station building sold out, they sent a rush of orders to get it in. Some students ran to buy it from other bookstores, while many others purchased it online.

"Thank you, Musubu, thank you!"

Overcome with emotion, Mayu Mayu grasped my hands and pumped them up and down.

Two weeks passed before I heard from Mayu Mayu that he had been officially notified by his head editor of the cancellation of *Steam from Another World ☆ The Great Giggling Battle—How a NEET like Me Reincarnated in Another World, Used My New Superpowers to Excavate a Hot Spring, and Formed a Harem!*

We were in a sitting area of the station building when he told me that sales of *The Great Giggling Battle* had exploded in one very small region, but the book hadn't made a dent nationally.

They didn't have the sales figures to warrant putting out a sequel, and they made the decision to cancel the series.

"Oh no…"

When I had received a message from Mayu Mayu asking me to meet him after school because there was something he wanted to tell me, I was sure he was going to reveal that a sequel was in the works. Steamy and I had been ready to celebrate. Now, sitting on my lap, Steamy was equally shocked at the bad news.

"I'm sorry. I talked a big game, but I was completely out of my depth." I hung my head.

"Absolutely not! I'm extremely grateful to you, Musubu," said Mayu Mayu, grinning. "I got to see books that I wrote flying off the shelves right before my eyes. My dream became a reality. And for the first time ever, the title of my book and my pen name made it onto the weekly sales list posted in the front window of the bookstore. I took a picture as a memento!"

This was the first time I had ever seen Mayu Mayu so bubbly.

He also showed me screenshots he had taken of online book reviews, where he had received many delighted reactions.

* * *

A super-fun read! The plot develops quickly, and it was exciting!

Easy to read, I finished the whole thing before I knew it. The girls are cute and comforting. I want to read it again.

The foreshadowing has me so curious… Can't wait for the next one!

This was the first time I read one of Mayu Sasaki's books, but it was all-engrossing. I'll definitely buy the next one. I'll be so happy if it picks up where this volume left off!

As he showed me one image at a time on the small screen of his smartphone, Mayu Mayu was smiling broadly, beaming with happiness.

He kept going on about how delighted he was and how this was the treasure of a lifetime.

"Also, look, there was stuff like this, too."

The next picture he showed me with a grin was a group photo of kids in cool poses or holding up peace signs, showing off the covers of their copies of *The Great Giggling Battle*. They wore Seijou Academy uniforms, so maybe it had been taken on campus?

The photo was tagged: *The book taking our school by storm! A super-fun story!*

There were also photographs of the book posed with stylish mugs, delicious-looking pancakes, and cute stuffed animals.

"I think this is the first time in my seven years as an author that one of my books has been enjoyed and loved so much. I've never felt like this before. It may have gotten canceled in the end, but I'm glad I wrote it. This book got to live a really happy life, I think."

From my lap, Steamy added, **"Mm, that's right, Mayu Mayu. Everyone seems to be having lots of fun. They seem so happy."**

For a book, there was no greater joy than knowing that the person turning your pages was enjoying themselves.

The pictures Mayu Mayu had shown me were all overflowing with a warm sense of joy, and the books in the photos all looked happy and lively.

"I won't be able to publish it, but I'm thinking about writing the sequel and making it available online. I want to do something to give back to all these people who have loved my book so much. Besides, someone from another publisher who read the new releases got in touch with me and suggested I try writing it at home. Apparently, he saw my book being posted on social media and read it out of curiosity. He told me the book's pacing was outstanding and said he definitely wanted to work together sometime."

"Amazing! That's great, Mayu Mayu!"

"That's wonderful news!"

Both Steamy and I raised our voices in delight.

After he giggled bashfully, a peaceful look came over Mayu Mayu's face. He stared into my eyes as he spoke.

"I had made up my mind to give up writing if I got canceled this time. But now I've decided to keep trying. It's all thanks to you, Musubu. Thank you."

After that, there was a bit of a light novel boom around Seijou Academy.

To my surprise, I even found Haruto in the conference room of the music hall reading a light novel with a girl on the cover.

"It's quite interesting."

He recommended it to me. It was Mayu Mayu's previous book, which Haruto had gone to the trouble of ordering online.

Apparently, Haruto had taken a liking to *Steam from Another World ☆ The Great Giggling Battle—How a NEET like Me Reincarnated in Another World, Used My New Superpowers to Excavate a Hot Spring, and Formed a Harem!* after all.

Mayu Mayu was working on the sequel to *The Great Giggling Battle* concurrently with writing his newest original work.

Steamy was still at my house.

I was having her stay on the bookshelf in my older sister's room, where I peeked in on her from time to time.

Whenever I was in a bad mood or feeling worn out, I went to secretly chat with Steamy while leafing through her as a pick-me-up.

Ah, I bet this must count as cheating, huh?

I felt a small sense of guilty pleasure as both Steamy and I looked forward to the day when Mayu Mayu would release the next part of *The Great Giggling Battle* online.

PRINCESS YONAGA'S INNER THOUGHTS

Absolutely must not be relayed to Musubu!

...The scent of another book was coming from Musubu.

Σ(°□°;)!!

...The smell of a hot spring.

(´・ω・`)

...He got into a hot spring bath with another book?!

o(*≧Д≦)o"

...Curse, curse, curse × 10,000,000,000.

ヾ(`ε´)ノヾ(`ε´)ノヾ(`ε´)ノヾ(`ε´)ノ(´_`。)(ノД•。)

...I—I would let Musubu read me in the bath, y'know.

。•°° ℩°(*/□*) ℩°° °•。

Book 3

A Book No One Knows, Viewed Upside Down

"Musubu... Hey, Mu-su-bu!"

A not-so-angelic voice called out close enough to brush the edge of my ear. Though sinister, obscene, and chilling all at once, I couldn't help but be charmed by it.

Ah, what a lovely voice it is.

Frightening yet enchanting, it might have belonged to, say, the devilish daughter of a noble—someone who would ecstatically drain every drop of lifeblood from a snake she had cut up, then dangle its corpse from a high building, wearing a sweet smile all the while.

An image of a beautiful girl with long, glossy black hair and a slim body, her bloodred lips moving as she call out to me, floated into my mind. I shivered all the way down to my fingertips.

"Do you love me? Musubu?"

Of course I do, no doubt about it.

Instead of answering, I gently traced the word *princess* with my index finger over her cover. I touched it ever so lightly, so lightly it wasn't clear whether I was really touching her at all.

She let out a small sigh, as if she were stirring slightly. She was like a black kitten that was narrowing its eyes and purring.

"Hey? Do you love me? Musubu. Do you care about me? Are you in love with me?"

She repeated her question in a slightly curt and arrogant voice, prodding me for an answer.

Recently, she had been acting spoiled a lot.

It's probably because she suspects me of keeping a mistress named Steamy in another room.

As a princess, she had a lot of pride, so I absolutely had not said anything about it to her. Nevertheless, she still burned with a sense of rivalry against Steamy, and she seemed to want me to reaffirm that I loved her more than the other book.

Last night, too, when I had started to leave the room to go take a bath, she had spoken up with uncharacteristic restlessness.

"Y-you... You could take me with you, if you'd like."

"Huh? But won't it be boring, waiting in the changing room?"

"......Mm."

After a brief silence, she returned a reply both chilly and bashful.

"I could go w-with you... You could take me in, with...you."

"Huh?! You want to get in the bath together? You'll let me read you in the bath? Wow, that would be the greatest! Wait, hang on a sec. You got me all hot and bothered for a moment there. If you get into the bath with me, the steam will wrinkle up all your pages."

"W-wrinkle...up?"

The image of the princess with long black hair returned to my mind's eye, and she seemed to be on the verge of tears.

"Besides, imagine if I slipped and dropped you into the water?"

"!"

* * *

She gasped, more afraid than before.

This was the girl who so disliked water that even when we were just walking outside, she would demand I put her inside my clothes and protect her if a single raindrop fell from the sky. I imagined she would feel nothing but fear and anxiety in a bathroom with a full tub.

Despite that, she put on her bravest front and insisted:

"If you wrap me neatly in a plastic bag so I don't get wet...I'll be fine."

"But if I do that, I can't read you."

"W-well, in that case, you should hold on to me carefully so that you don't drop me."

No matter what I told her might happen, she wouldn't give up on the idea of bathing with me, so—

"All right, just for a little while."

I headed for the bathroom, cradling her in my arms.

Even while I undressed in the changing room, she trembled. She was obviously frightened. Once I was naked, I carefully picked her up in both hands and gently wrapped her in a towel. She was still quivering. After that, she went silent, as if she were holding her breath.

"You don't have to force yourself. I know you're probably concerned about Steamy and all, but you're the only one I love, Princess Yonaga, and I'm not getting in the bath with any other books, her included."

"Th-that's...got nothing to do with this."

"Sure, but..."

* * *

Her fear was obvious. When I hesitated to take her in with me, she said something in a voice filled with desperate resolve that threatened to move me to tears.

"B-besides...if you haven't gotten into the bath with any other books, then that would make me your...first."

Oh, that really got me going. My heart pounded in my chest, and my face grew hot, even though I wasn't soaking in the bath yet. *My girlfriend is too cute.*

"Understood. I'll protect you."

I brought my face in close to the book and whispered to her in a manly way, then stepped into the steam-filled bathroom with her in my arms.

"Ohhh."

She let out an adorable moan. As I sank into the hot water, she chastised me:

"You mustn't drop me! It would be absolutely awful if you dropped me, you know."

"It's all right. Trust me."

She made a bashful squeak as I gently unwound the towel from her slim body. To reduce the effects of the steam somewhat, I placed the towel I had just taken off her onto the side of the bathtub and laid Princes Yonaga down on top of it.

"All right, I'm reading."

"Mm-hmm..."

* * *

"Let's take it slow today, okay?"

"Mm-hmm..."

Encouraging the nervous, trembling book the whole while, I turned her pages even more gently and carefully than usual.

Ah! To think that the day has come when I can read my beloved girlfriend in the bath. I could almost see the indigo princess blushing pink.

So as not to tax her too much, I stayed in the bath for only a short while. Still, it was a very intense experience for both of us.

"We smell the same..."

After I went back to my room, the princess, enveloped in the scent of my bath salts, mumbled softly to herself from atop my bed, making me swoon all over again.

"Was I...your first, Musubu?"

Such an adorable question, whispered in such a delicate, bashful voice. I squeezed her tight against my chest.

"Of course you were. You're my one and only love, Princess Yonaga."

"I love you, Musubu. I really do."

She sounded genuinely happy as she graced me with words she usually never let slip.

Today, an aftertaste of that shared joy still lingered, and she continued pleading with me.

"Come on, tell me out loud—tell me you love me!"

But we're at school...

I broke into a grin while tracing the word with my finger, *princess, princess, princess…*

"You have to say it...or I'll cut off your ears!" she threatened.

Augh! I just can't handle that she can have such childish voice and sound so arrogant at the same time, I thought. *I'm liable to follow any order she gives! Well, it's probably fine… I'm sure no one can hear me right now. I bet I can say it. Yeah. I'm saying it.*

"I love you…"

Suddenly, the image of the princess vanished before my eyes.

"So sorry, but this is an emergency."

In front of the desk, in place of the slim book with the indigo cover—in place of my beloved Princess Yonaga—stood a tall, handsome boy. The third-year student whom everyone called the Campus Prince, Haruto Himekura.

"It's not often that you come to my classroom, Haruto. You usually send me a message over LINE or a text."

"I sent you something over LINE, but you didn't read it, so I figured you were enjoying your time with your girlfriend and wouldn't answer your phone for a while. Thus, I had to come in person."

It was lunchtime. I was following Haruto to the music hall after he had crushed the fleeting, tender moment I'd shared with my girlfriend.

Inside the music hall were all the orchestra clubrooms. Haruto had served as conductor for the orchestra club since his first year at the school.

Usually, when I had something to discuss with Haruto, we did it in the conference room of the music hall. We talked there because no one would overhear our more…complicated conversations.

Today, too, we sat across from each other on expensive-looking leather sofas, and Haruto quickly launched into the topic at hand.

"Do you know Takanari Wakasako, a first-year in the orchestra club? The one who caused a bit of an uproar around school lately?"

"Sorry, I'm not up on current events."

"Right, I ought to know by now that you live in a different dimension from everyone else, Musubu."

He probably meant that as soon as I started turning the pages of a book, my surroundings faded away as I let myself be absorbed in conversation with it. In fact, my special ability to hear the voices of books was the whole reason a commoner like me sat here conversing casually with the Campus Prince.

Haruto proceeded to tell me about this Wakasako person.

He played cello in the orchestra club, was a serious and diligent student, got good grades, and was trusted by his peers.

In the middle of orchestra practice the day before, he had suddenly launched a furious verbal attack against all the second-year students.

"They were just using the club's copier to photocopy some notes they had borrowed from another second-year club member. All of a sudden, he ripped the plug out of the wall and told everyone off, accusing them of cheating. Everyone was flabbergasted."

"That's cheating, isn't it?! Stop it right now!"

"Huh? Wakasako, what are you talking about?"

"All of it, it's all crooked! Using club equipment to make personal copies and copying another person's assignment to hand in as your own! It's evil!"

"Okay, weirdo…"

Sure, you could technically argue that plagiarizing someone else's assignment isn't right, but everyone does it. Even I've written book reports for people in exchange for copying their summer homework assignments. It's not something a first-year would normally go out of his way to chastise upperclassmen about.

The upperclassmen had seemed more taken aback than angry at the usually quiet Wakasako's indignant outburst.

But he hadn't stopped there.

Later on, after school, Wakasako had suddenly taken off running down a hallway while shouting in a strange voice.

"By night—I'll be eaten by night!"

His eyes had been bloodshot and his hair disheveled as he yelled, and he sprinted down the hallway from end to end, until he collapsed with a crash and had to be carried off to the health room. That was yesterday.

"'I'll be eaten by night'…? What does that mean?" I asked.

Haruto shook his head. "I talked a little with Wakasako when he arrived at school this morning, but he says his head suddenly heated up like it was boiling over and that he doesn't remember anything after that. It was the same when he scolded the upperclassmen—all he could tell me was that his head got hot and he had a feeling that what they were doing was 'unacceptable.' Wakasako himself seemed frightened by his own behavior."

Haruto told me that when he asked Wakasako if anything had changed in his life recently or if he was troubled by anything, Wakasako had cast his eyes downward and answered:

"Five days ago, in the school library after classes, my head suddenly got hot, and I collapsed… The next day was Saturday, and I went to the hospital to get checked out, but nothing was out of order."

"He collapsed in the library…?"

I see—so that's why I've been summoned.

"That's right, the library. The place where tens of thousands of books reside. This is where you come in, right, Musubu? Besides, there's the matter of repaying the favor I did for Mr. Sasaki."

He was right. When I had requested Haruto's cooperation to sell Mayu Mayu's newest book, I had been warned that the debt would be considerable.

"Got it—I'll take the job. I'd like to hear Wakasako's side of the story first, though…"

And so, Haruto summoned Wakasako to the library after school, where the whole incident had started.

"What will we talk about with him, Haruto?"

"I wonder if he'll provide us with more details about when he collapsed here."

Wakasako had a slim build, eyes that smiled, and a clever look about him. He leaned his cheek against his right hand and regarded us suspiciously.

I had expected as much. He had been expressly summoned to the library, which had been reserved through Haruto's connections, and now some stranger was standing in front of him as if he owned the place.

"Sorry, but who is this guy?"

He scrutinized me cautiously.

"Musubu knows a lot about books. He's often passing through the library, so I thought he might know something, and I asked him to come."

"Nice to meet you. I'm Musubu Enoki. I'm in the same grade as you, first year, Class 1."

"...Hi."

Wakasako squinted at me with even greater suspicion.

From the look in his eyes, I could tell he was wondering how the fact that I knew a lot about books and went to the library often was supposed to help.

Perhaps he tended to be brusque, because he repositioned his right hand almost as if to hide his own face and quickly averted his eyes from me, then responded curtly, "I told you everything yesterday. I came to do some research in the library, then my head heated up, and I fainted. That's it."

I spoke up. "At that time, were you reading any particular book?"

"...I don't remember."

"All right, where did you collapse? Let's try going there."

For some reason, Wakasako didn't seem be in the mood to listen to what I had to say, but when Haruto pressed him on, Wakasako rubbed his hand over his face again and started walking reluctantly.

We went past the study area with its neat rows of tables and chairs and headed into a section of the library where the bookshelves towered over us like a forest. Squeezing between the many volumes packed tight onto the shelves, we proceeded deeper into the stacks.

The library at Seijou Academy was as large as a university library and housed a vast collection of books. You couldn't reach the top shelves just by stretching your arms up, so stepladders had been placed around the room.

If an earthquake were to occur at this moment, we would likely be entombed in massive quantities of paper and ink. For just for a moment, I was absorbed in the thought that that would be a very happy death indeed.

I might be a little too *into books.*

"Musubu, whose story did you come to read today?"

Oh, I hear a voice calling out to me.

"It's me, isn't it, Musubu?"

"Musubuuu, it's time you got around to reading us!"

I listened carefully to the many voices reaching out to me from the shelves.

"What's up, Musubu? You look so solemn—what happened?"
"Heh-heh, three boys having a secret meeting in the library?"
"You don't have your crazy-jealous girlfriend with you today?"

I can hear the voices of books.

The loudest and most fiercely insistent are the shiny new publications piled up in bookstores. Books in the library are usually pretty calm, though sometimes one will ask hopefully if I'm tired and need something to read during a break from my studies.

Maybe the books were livelier than usual because I hadn't visited the library in a while.

"The tall, handsome boy with Musubu is the Campus Prince, you know!"

"It's true. Once, a girl with long, beautiful hair confessed her love to him right before my eyes. She was devastated when he turned her down."

"Before that girl, there was the sexy teacher with the mole by her mouth. Man, did she complain about it when the prince artfully brushed off her advances."

Well, this is awkward. I'm not here to find out about the state of Haruto's love life. But the sexy teacher with the mole by her mouth? That's got to be the music teacher... No, no, I've got to let it go.

I pretended I hadn't heard anything, and we proceeded ever deeper.

Eventually, Wakasako ground to a halt near the shelves that held collections of modern Japanese literature. "I think it was around here," he said bluntly over his shoulder.

Kouyou Ozaki, Shimei Futabatei, Saneatsu Mushanokouji, Souseki Natsume, Ryūnosuke Akutagawa, Osamu Dazai...it was a meeting of the literary masters.

All these books had stood the test of time, and their voices were as dignified as their weighty, imposing appearances. However, they didn't chatter like the other books, preferring to keep to themselves...until something happened.

Suddenly, I heard a sharp shriek deep in my ear that pierced me to the core.

"I'm scared!"

"There are so many corpses!"

"We'll be eaten by the darkness!"

What? What's this?

The books were astir.

So many voices combined and competed with one another that I couldn't tell which titles they belonged to. Their cries echoed together inside my mind.

All the voices seemed singularly obsessed with something, and it made the hair stand up on the back of my neck and sent a cold shudder up my spine.

I had only experienced books shouting over one another in a whirlwind of fear like this once before. It was during that terrifying, sorrowful, blood-soaked incident—

The voices stacked one on top of the other, and the cacophony intensified.

"The crows!"

"The bodies are just—"

"No one knows they're here."

"No one, no one, no one—"

Oh no, they're dragging me in!

Against a bright-red background that made it look as if the backs of my eyeballs had been doused in blood, I saw black crows circling countless corpses spread out on the ground. The sweet and sour scent of death hit the back of my throat and made me gag. I could feel bittersweet saliva accumulating in my mouth, as if I was about to throw up, when I noticed that someone beside me had already dropped to his knees before I did.

It was Wakasako.

As he shielded the right side of his face with his palm, his eyes were wide with fear. His whole body shook violently, and his breathing was ragged. A hoarse voice escaped from his quivering lips.

"I'll be *devoured*… I'll be *swallowed up*…"

His wide-open eyes gradually turned red, and his voice trembled uncontrollably as he bent backward to look up at the ceiling and release a terrible shriek.

Haruto knelt down on the floor, grabbed Wakasako by both shoulders, and peered into his face. "Wakasako, are you all right?!"

He met Wakasako's eyes with a strong, direct gaze. Wakasako had placed his hand over the right side of his face and had been panting, but now his breathing calmed a little as the look of madness faded from his eyes.

"It was foolish of me to force you to return to the very spot where something so awful happened. Let's go to the nurse's office."

"No...um...I'm fine. I'm sorry for losing my composure. I don't know why, but my head suddenly got hot again..." With assistance from Haruto, Wakasako stood up.

Still concerned, Haruto asked, "You said, 'I'll be devoured.' Does that jog your memory at all?"

Wakasako hung his head weakly and place his right hand on his cheek.

Ah...again.

That same gesture.

"I said that? I'm sorry. I don't remember..."

"It's all right. I'm sure you're just tired. You usually try so hard to be considerate of others. Seems like you'd better go home and rest today, after all. I'll send you with my driver."

Wakasako tried countless times to turn down the favor, but in the end, Haruto overcame his reluctance. "Consider it an order from an upperclassman."

The whole time this was going on, the books were whispering like a bunch of ghosts gathered in a graveyard.

"There are so many corpses."
"The crows are coming for the bodies."

"The darkness—the night—"

◇ ◇ ◇

"I think Wakasako has been *infected by the books*."

Once Wakasako had been placed under the care of the Himekura family's personal driver, Haruto and I returned to the conference room of the music hall.

Casting down his eyes with a look of distress, Haruto mumbled, "That's got to be it."

Both Haruto and I had witnessed people falling ill with symptoms similar to Wakasako's before.

Book sickness.

I suspect that many people have experienced a mild form of this malady. It occurs when someone reads a book and goes too deep into the world of the text, entering a trancelike state where they can't quite manage to come back to reality. Almost as if a part of their mind is stuck inside the story. They feel the sorrows, hardships, and joys of the characters as their own.

If you fell under the influence of the novel *Daddy-Long-Legs*, you would start writing down every little thing about your daily life in a letter and hide in the shadows to watch over a girl who interested you. That would constitute a less-dangerous manifestation of the illness.

But it would be far more serious if you were infected by *The Stranger* and were driven to kill someone because the sun was in your eyes, for instance.

The infected individual Haruto and I had encountered before had thought he and the character in the book were one and the same. He honestly believed he had done something terrible.

Just thinking about it made my stomach twist in knots. The memory of that incident still deeply scarred my heart, and I didn't want anything like that to happen ever again. If Wakasako had lost himself under the influence of some book, I knew I had to do my utmost to assist him.

No, not only Wakasako. I wanted to help the book that had become the source of this trouble through no fault of its own—

"Somehow or other, we've got to identify the book causing the illness. I'm going back to the library to ask around. Please tell me anything else you know about Wakasako."

Haruto must be feeling the same way as me.

We can't let something like that happen ever again.

Never again!

Haruto looked soberly into my eyes. "Understood. I'll try not to let Wakasako out of my sight."

"Musubu...I don't want you to get involved with this."

That night—

As I sat at my desk at home, intently devouring the data Haruto had sent me on my phone about Wakasako, Princess Yonaga beseeched me again and again in frigid, sensuous tones from where she sat behind me on the bed.

"...It sounds like the book that infected this boy contains many references to corpses... It's dangerous... Besides, if the other books around it are the same type, then... Musubu, you too...might get... drawn in and infected..."

"I'll be fine. I'll be careful so that won't happen."

"...Musubu, because you can hear the voices of books...it's easy for your emotions to get away from you... Far easier than it is for a normal human... Remember that time before..."

"Only I can hear the voices of books and people alike, so only I can stop anything like that from happening again. I can't just *not* do something. Both Wakasako and the book causing this must be in terrible agony."

Wasn't it the same for you?

I didn't say that part out loud, but Princess Yonaga must also have been thinking about her own complicated history. She remained silent.

"..."

Then, in a feeble voice, she muttered, "...I don't care...about some other book. Even if every other book and person in the world were destroyed, I wouldn't mind so long as you were safe..."

Her scenario bordered on absurdity, but I was sure she was really just worried about me.

"Thanks. But this is my role to play."

For as long as I can remember, I have been able to hear the voices of books just like those of any other. I've always thought that surely there must be some meaning to it, some grander purpose.

That was why I couldn't ignore any voice, no matter how small.

I spun my chair around to face Princess Yonaga and smiled resolutely. "I am a voice for books, after all."

My anxious girlfriend let out an overburdened groan. "...I hate when you're thinking about other books... Musubu."

I looked back at my phone and continued to read, but she kept on weeping. "...I hate it...Musubu... I hate it...hate it...utterly hate it...!"

I'd better sort this out quickly to put Princess Yonaga's mind at ease...

I proceeded to memorize all the information on Wakasako. His stellar grades in middle school had allowed him to gain admittance to the famous private school Seijou Academy, where he maintained his position at the top of his class. Among his classmates, he tended to be a sort of peacekeeper, and even second- and third-year upperclassmen sometimes relied on his help.

His hobbies are— Huh? Math? This says he got third place for participating in a nationwide mental math competition when he was in middle school... Incredible. I'm sure he must be quite a logical person. Just what kind of book could cause an infection that would make someone like that start running around the halls shouting in strange voices and lashing out at upperclassmen for copying someone else's assignment?

Let's start there.

If we can't identify the source of the disease, then a cure will be hard to come by.

Let me think back on what Wakasako blurted out in the library, along with whatever those books were muttering about.

"*I'll be* devoured... *I'll be* swallowed up..."

"By the night—I'll be eaten by night!"

The key word was *night*.

Be swallowed up by night?

And then there were the "corpses."

"There are so many corpses."

"The bodies are just— The bodies—"

"No one knows they're here."

The vision I saw lined up with what the books were saying. Bodies piled up in a heap in the darkness. A murder of black crows dotting the red sky.

Hmm, a novel that depicts corpses scattered about everywhere, giving off the stench of death...

It reminded me a great deal of the indigo book who was watching me from behind like a teary-eyed girl, with bitter anxiety. Fortunately, she contained images of swarming snakes, not a flock of crows.

I got the feeling Wakasako's lashing out at the upperclassmen was genuine. Moreover, it stemmed from anger rather than fear.

"Anger," huh...?

That's probably another key word.

So then, what could Wakasako be angry about?

What was so unacceptable, exactly?

A story about an angry man...? With corpses scattered about? And crows...?

The title felt as if it was on the tip of my tongue, but it wouldn't come to me.

The following morning, I went to the library again before classes started and stood before the modern Japanese literature section to ask the books whether they knew anything about the novel that could have infected Wakasako.

"I don't know," a voice whispered.

"I don't know," another added.

That was all I really got.

"No one knows."

"We don't know."

"Dunno."

"Do as you please, just leave me out of it."

The voices reverberating from all around me kept coming faster and louder, so I left for class without a single clue to go on, much less a title.

Corpses...corpses... Ugh, I really wish I had more to go on than that.

I puzzled over dead bodies and the smell of death all throughout lunch like some sort of creep, while Princess Yonaga anxiously interrogated me from inside my pocket.

"Musubu...you're zoning out, and your glasses are all askew... It's strange. Did you get...infected?"

I hurried to adjust my glasses, then turned to Princess Yonaga and whispered, "Look, I'm not infected, okay? Ah, let's eat outside for a little change of pace, shall we?"

I left the classroom carrying my mother's homemade lunch.

Well then, where should we go?

Walking down the hallway in thought, I caught sight of Wakasako. In one hand, he carried a bag from the school canteen.

I jogged to close the distance between us. "Wakasako! Are you going to lunch now?" I asked. "Wanna eat together?"

"Musubu, no!"

From my pocket, Princess Yonaga voiced her objection.

Sorry, I promise to read you once this incident is cleared up.

"You are…?"

"Musubu Enoki. First year, Class 1, student number eight. My hobby is reading, my special skill is reading, and I spend my weekends browsing bookstores or libraries and reading at home."

Wakasako looked at me as if I were some sort of alien when I launched into a full self-introduction there in the hallway, but then I told him, "Haruto asked me to help with your situation. There's something I'd like to ask you, so would you come with me for a bit?"

He accepted, despite an obvious lack of enthusiasm.

The timid voice of Princess Yonaga escaped from my pocket. **"Imbecile... I hate you... I'll set a curse upon you!"**

We sat beside each other on a bench outside. The courtyard at Seijou Academy had been styled in the image of an English garden and featured a rose arch and a flower clock.

The mid-July sun was dazzling, but the tree branches above our heads provided comfortable shade, and the breeze was cool. This spot had been the right choice.

"Are you feeling all right now?"

"...Yeah. I feel bad for making Haruto worry about me, though."

"Don't let it bother you. He likes taking care of people."

Though Haruto, too, had a dark side, he was fundamentally a gentleman. The type of person who never failed to lend a hand if he saw someone in trouble, who personally safeguarded the peace at the school. That's why he was always sticking his nose into this, that, and the other and setting up jobs for me.

"Enoki, you're...really close to Haruto, huh? You're in different clubs, so how do you know each other? I was wondering, are you, like, his relative or something?"

"No, no. My family is descended from generations of commoners. We don't have any relation to such a distinguished lineage. Look, even my lunch is utterly ordinary."

I showed him my unimpressive lunch box containing a rolled omelet, some fried stuff left over from last night's dinner, broccoli salad, and rice with a pickled plum on top. Wakasako seemed to let down his guard a bit.

"Books brought Haruto and me together. He's quite the reader as well. I guess you could say we're book buddies."

It wasn't a lie, exactly. Though I had altered a few details.

"Is that so?"

Wakasako seemed to understand, but he still appeared somewhat restless. He placed his hand on the right side of his face and muttered, "...So you wanted to ask me something?"

"Right, you said you don't remember whether you were reading a book when you collapsed in the library, right?"

"Yeah."

According to Haruto, Wakasako had grabbed a bookshelf as he collapsed, and the books that had fallen off had scattered around the area.

The librarian who had found Wakasako didn't remember any of the titles, but he had fallen in front of the modern Japanese literature section, so it was most likely a book from somewhere around there.

"What were you looking for in the library?" I asked.

"An assignment came up in my class to write a haiku, so I thought I would find a few to reference."

"Ah, we had that assignment in my class, too. You're a real serious student, going out of your way to research before you write. But the poetry section where the haiku books are is three shelves past the Japanese literature section."

"Oh…is it?"

"Why were you lying in front of the Japanese literature anthologies?"

"I don't usually use the school library much, so I don't have a great sense for which books are where. I must have ended up there by accident."

"Hmm, guess so."

It's easy enough to end up wandering around areas outside the section you're looking for in an unfamiliar library or bookshop.

"What kind of books do you like, Wakasako?"

"What books do I like?" Wakasako looked as though he didn't quite understand the intent of my question. "I don't read anything besides textbooks. I prefer numbers to words. Well, if there were a book filled with nothing but rows of numbers, I'd probably like reading it, I guess."

A book with lots of numbers, eh…? Hmm…I suppose there must be some people in this world who think lists of numbers might make a decent novel, but I can't even begin to imagine how a person would act if they got infected by a book like that.

Maybe they would suddenly start writing out equations in chalk on the hallway walls? But I have a feeling they wouldn't prance around shouting in a strange voice about being "swallowed up" by night.

"By the way, I heard you took third place at a national mental-math competition. That's impressive. How many digits do you think you can calculate in your head?"

"My best is sixteen."

"Sixteen digits! That's without using a calculator—you just look at the problem and answer? You must be a genius."

"It's not all that impressive. If you picture an abacus in your mind and use the beads to do your calculations, anyone can do it."

"No, I doubt it. I can't even do two-digit addition without writing it down on paper. You're really amazing!"

"...That's not true."

Wakasako didn't seem very enthused, even while being praised. My genuine amazement didn't seem to matter to him.

"From my perspective, placing third in the country is amazing. Besides that, Haruto tells me you're the manager for the first-years in the orchestra club and that the upperclassmen depend on you for stuff, too."

Out of nowhere, a flash of savage emotion crossed Wakasako's eyes. Anger, annoyance, dissatisfaction, frustration—all those emotions jostled together and let sparks fly.

He pressed his palm tight against his own right cheek, as if trying to hold back some destructive urge.

As he was doing that, he spoke low enough to growl. "No one depends on me for anything."

"Huh? But—"

"I was not recommended for the role of manager."

His expression darkened, as if obscured by a gray cloud.

I gulped. "The role of manager?" I asked.

With his hand on his right cheek, he looked down at his feet.

"In the orchestra club, aside from the club president and the director, there are leaders for each instrument section and leaders for each grade. The grade leaders are called managers. During the first semester, the second-year leader was also in charge of the first-years, but at the start of the second semester, one first-year student was selected to take over the job, on the recommendation of the second- and third-year members. The selection took place last week. I was not recommended by anyone, so I'm not the manager."

Wakasako's lips curled in mortification. A shadow fell over the area below his downturned eyes, making him seem even more miserable.

"Is it really such an important position?"

"...Every year, the club president is chosen from among the managers. So I have to become a manager first."

"You want to be orchestra club president, Wakasako?"

"If I can list 'president of the orchestra club at Seijou Academy' on my resume, I'll be able to get a direct recommendation into any university I want."

He smiled in self-deprecation, as though he wondered why he was explaining all this to a guy he had just met.

To become the orchestra club president, he would have to first assume the post of first-year manager. And to do that, he needed the backing of the upperclassmen—hence his inability to become a manager. He probably felt that coveted university recommendation slipping further and further away.

"Your grades are top of the class, too, aren't they? With that kind of standing, at a school like ours, you should be able to apply anywhere you want, even if you have to take the exam like everyone else."

"People told me that in middle school, too. 'With your grades, you're sure to get in anywhere,' they said. But that didn't turn out to be true. In fact, I failed spectacularly at getting into my first-choice high school."

Oh really…?

But Seijou Academy is a well-known and exclusive college prep school, outfitted with facilities on par with a university, though there are *ultra-high-level prep schools with superior academic standings. My mom always complains about tuition being too high…*

I imagined the school Wakasako had his eye on in middle school was one of those ultra-competitive schools. After being told he would definitely succeed, I bet he failed to score high enough and ended up at our school. Since the orchestra club had a reputation for getting its members strong recommendations, he must have joined to secure an ironclad resume.

Wakasako seemed like a hardworking person, so I was sure he steadily gained the trust of the upperclassmen. But for whatever reason, he couldn't get them to back him for the position of manager, the leader of the first-year students. As an outsider, I couldn't begin to guess why.

What a shocking situation…

* * *

Considering his feelings made my own chest throb with pain. "Well… now the stage is set for your comeback. From my perspective, taking third at a mental-math competition is plenty amazing. I think you're brilliant."

"The guy who got first place mentioned offhand in his victory interview that he doesn't even practice regularly. His talent is on a totally different level from mine. I work and work and work and only make it as far as third place. A guy like that was born a genius. Me? I'm…ordinary. I've got no future."

Wakasako's voice was like a dark night right before it rains, clammy and gloomy. Then he fell completely silent, the palm of his hand still glued to his right cheek.

How can he say he's got no future?

He's only fifteen or sixteen, still in his first year of high school!

His grades were outstanding, he wasn't bad looking, and he was taller than me. He put in effort at club activities every day, and he had a goal in mind. Compared with Wakasako, I was a boring four-eyed baby face, and I probably wasn't getting taller any time soon. I spent my days self-indulgently absorbed in the world of books, and if I could, I'd spend the rest of my life leisurely reading. I'd be over the moon if I could shut myself away in a room filled with books to live out the rest of my days… Princess Yonaga would get jealous and insist she hated the other books being in there with us, but she was cute even when she was upset. *I'm such a weird guy for getting so worked up over wild delusions…*

"Augh!" My sudden cry startled Wakasako and caused him to lift his head. Princess Yonaga also gasped from inside my pocket.

"Wh-what happened?" Wakasako asked.

"You're worried about your future, with all you have going for you, but when I try to imagine what the future holds for a guy like me, who's not good for anything other than reading books—"

"What kind of future…do you see?"

"I envision myself lazing about, buried under books, reclining on a bed flooded with them! I see a recluse! A shut-in! This is bad! I'm in real trouble!"

Despite my genuine distress, Princess Yonaga was snarky as usual. **"Just die, then."** Wakasako regarded me blankly, his mouth hanging open.

He continued to stare, as if observing some mysterious creature, so I frowned as hard as I could and tried to look pitiful.

"Hey, what should I do?" I asked.

"I dunno," he quipped, unconcerned.

Then the bell rang, and lunchtime came to an end.

Wakasako had barely touched the bread he had purchased at the canteen.

"We didn't even get to eat. Sorry."

"It's fine. I didn't feel much like eating anyway," he replied, then put the bread back into its bag before returning to his own classroom.

His expression is softer than it was when I invited him to lunch, and he certainly seems to have lightened up, but…I don't think Wakasako's gotten over being left out of the recommendations for orchestra manager yet… Maybe that's related to the cause of his infection…

But I wonder—why wasn't Wakasako recommended in the first place? From everything Haruto's told me, he seems to be trusted by his peers.

From inside my pocket, Princess Yonaga spoke up.

"Musubu, are you imagining a future where you're buried in books other than me...? Is that what lurks in your heart? I'll curse, curse, curse, curse you!"

"Darkness mode" was back with a vengeance.

When I relayed the details of what I had discussed with Wakasako to Haruto in the conference room after school, he frowned.

"I see… So Wakasako is that consumed with not making manager, huh…? He always acted normal in front of everyone, but he did make all sorts of blunders, you know."

What kind of blunders?

Haruto grimaced, an expression uncharacteristic of him.

"I thought Wakasako was one of the front-runners, wasn't he?" I asked. "Why didn't he get the recommendation?"

"Ah, well, I also considered him a favorite," Haruto replied. "But right before the selection was made, an unsavory rumor spread about him."

"What rumor?"

"It goes that, back in middle school, Wakasako pushed a classmate off a second-story veranda, seriously injuring him..."

"What, straitlaced Wakasako? No way."

"Apparently, several other boys were there when their classmate went flying off the veranda. But Wakasako was trying to stop them from bullying the other boy. He didn't do the pushing."

"So then why is that rumor going around? Is that what caused him to miss out on the recommendation?"

"Exactly. Club members supporting a rival candidate seemed to have conjured up the story, pretending it was gossip. Dammit, if only I had realized sooner!" Haruto was genuinely vexed.

Haruto always acts like nothing fazes him, but I guess even a prince has his limits... He's still a third-year in high school, so I suppose that's only natural.

"Do you think Wakasako knows he didn't get the position because of the rumor?"

"I wonder..."

If he did know, he was probably devasted. I imagine he felt anger and emptiness.

"...I've got no future."

Wakasako must have felt hopeless in the face of everything, hopeless enough to let those words slip from his anguished face.

So snapping suddenly at the upperclassmen might also have been...

"That's cheating, isn't it?! Stop it right now!"

Having lost his chance because of foul play, the smallest act of unfairness must have infuriated him. Or maybe the upperclassmen making copies of their assignments were the perpetrators who had spread the rumor?

"That's cheating, *isn't it?!"*

* * *

A protagonist who loathes dishonesty...

Something clicked in the back of my mind.

Ah...I can almost see it.

Just then, a spine-chilling voice emanated from my bag.

"Upside down..."

A voice equal parts enticing, horrific, and haughty—a devilish voice.

I looked down in terror at the school backpack by my side.

Was that Princess Yonaga...?

I was just talking to Haruto. I wasn't being unfaithful. Wait, no, this voice *feels like—*

"...Saw everything...upside down..."

This lifeless utterance, devoid of any emotion, was the same as the voices that had spoken in chorus in the library—*and the same as the voice from that time—*

Fingers unsteady, I unzipped my bag. I pulled out the slim volume with the indigo cover and held it in both hands, then brought my face so close to it that my glasses almost touched it.

"Princess Yonaga, it's me! It's Musubu! Can you hear me?"

People contract book sickness when they were too fully absorbed in the world of the book. And books could get sick, too—through contact with an infected person, the source book could imprint on their minds and enchant them just the same.

Princess Yonaga had been there to hear my conversation with Wakasako in the garden today, so maybe now she was resonating with the problem book, just as the other books in the library had?

Meanwhile, Haruto stared dumbstruck at his friend suddenly shouting at a book.

"Princess Yonaga. Can you hear me? Answer me!"

"I don't know you."

*   *   *

All the blood drained from my face when I heard the hollow voice.

"I don't associate with cheaters... I loathe them. Hmph!"

I heaved a sigh of relief at Princess Yonaga's adorable protest, grateful she was her usual self.

"Musubu, what did your girlfriend have to say?" Haruto inquired.

"Apparently, she loathes cheaters."

"...Do you think you could have your lovers' quarrels on your own time?"

Haruto looked exasperated, but I was glad Princess Yonaga had returned to normal. My heart nearly stopped when she said she didn't know me.

Hang on.

Come to think of it, the books in the library were chanting the same words.

"I don't know."

"No one knows."

"We don't know."

"Dunno."

"Do as you please, just leave me out of it."

And then there was what Princess Yonaga had indifferently grumbled about while resonating with Wakasako.

"Saw everything...upside down."

Upside down?

Reversal of good and evil.

A world reflected upside down.

Crows at twilight.

The darkness of night.

"No one knows."

"Haruto, has Wakasako always touched his cheek?"

"No, but now that you mention it, he has been doing it a lot lately."

Just as a light bulb went off in my head and a single title materialized in my mind, Haruto's smartphone vibrated.

As soon as he looked down at the screen, he stood up and started speaking with someone.

"I saw your message on LINE. How's Wakasako?"

Something must have happened to him!

Haruto's voice faltered, his expression turning stern. Urging me to follow with a flick of his head, he walked off as he continued his phone call.

My heart rate rose, and sweat oozed from my palms. As I was about to return Princess Yonaga to my backpack and follow behind Haruto, she called to me.

"Take me with you, too."

"But—"

But you might resonate with the book again.

"If you leave me behind, I'll never let you read me again."

I frantically tucked Princess Yonaga into my pocket and chased after Haruto.

As we descended in the elevator, Haruto grimly relayed to me the contents of his phone call.

"Sounds like Wakasako had another fight with the upperclassmen. They say he fled from the room shouting in a strange voice."

The same upperclassmen who had been trying to copy assignments earlier were trying to push their own duties in the orchestra club off onto the first-years.

Wakasako had overheard their exchange and had suddenly snapped at them again.

"I won't stand for dishonesty!"

"This is just normal stuff! Everyone does it, geez."

The moment one of the upperclassmen responded to him, Wakasako had started to shake violently and screamed peculiarly.

Then he'd thrown himself toward the upperclassman, violently ripped the other boy's uniform jacket and shirt, and fled the room grasping the clothes tight, all while spouting nonsense.

"It's normal! Totally normal!"

Haruto broke into a sprint as soon as the elevator doors opened, and I followed suit.

As we ran, another message came in with Wakasako's whereabouts. He had left the music hall and headed straight for the classroom building like a hurricane, dashing up the stairs with bloodshot eyes.

Up and—

—up and—

—up he went.

That's right. If the book that infected Wakasako is the one I think it is, he'll become obsessed with climbing higher and higher.

Just like the man in the story—in the rain, out of work, with no place to go. At a loss, he decides to finally break out of his hopeless stupor by climbing up and up, trying to get higher.

We were running at full speed, so my breath was strained. On top of that, I was getting dizzy, and I knew that if I lost focus, I would probably fall face-first on the floor.

The distance between Haruto and me widened.

Shit, get it together, legs!

My knees were leaden. I could barely lift them.

As I was on the verge of exploding with frustration, my shoulders heaving in time with my breaths, something whispered to me from my pocket,

"I don't know... I don't know..."

Perhaps I was resonating with the source of the voice, because a vision of a bloodred setting sun and crows scattered through the sky like black sesame seeds clouded my view.

Could Princess Yonaga be intentionally resonating with me in order to show me this?

The crows gradually joined all their hoarse voices into one, forming a black ring in the sky.

Below them stood an imposing gate and…

"…just a single cricket clinging to a huge red pillar from which the lacquer was peeling here and there."

Haruto was dashing up the stairs two at a time.

I could only take them one by one.

Up and up and up.

"To do something when there was nothing to be done, he would have to be prepared to do anything at all. If he hesitated, he would end up starving to death against an earthen wall or in the roadside dirt."

Haruto finally arrived at the door that led to the roof and thrust it open.

Once he climbed up, there before him, the corpses—

"Wakasakooo!"

Haruto's scream pierced my ears as I finished climbing the stairs, dripping with sweat.

"Come back, Wakasako!"

Haruto was calling out to him. When I finally emerged onto the roof, a damp breeze blew against my cheek. The sky was painted the red color of sunset, and the roof and water tower were also tinged a dull scarlet, like blood had been spilled everywhere.

My panting would not cease, and as I staggered forward and looked around, I spotted Wakasako hunched over, halfway up the water tower ladder.

Haruto was yelling at him to come down.

Even I shouted with all the volume I could muster, my shoulders heaving with every breath and my steps as unsteady as an old man's. "Wakasako! I figured out the title of the story you read in the library!"

Maybe he didn't hear me. He exhaled violently from his open mouth and clung to the ladder, face still stiff with fear.

"*You read Ryūnosuke Akutagawa's 'Rashōmon'!* Wakasako, you've been *infected by 'Rashōmon'*!"

Haruto turned around to look at me.

Wakasako's eyes were still locked on the sky. I wondered what he glimpsed in that moment.

A murder of crows, sprinkled like so many flying sesame seeds against a bloody evening sky?

A mountain of corpses, abandoned in the room at the top of a gatehouse?

"Wakasako, you told me you don't read any books other than your textbooks, but 'Rashōmon' is a famous story studied in school, so you must be familiar with it, right? On that day, when you visited the school library and passed in front of the literature anthologies, a copy containing 'Rashōmon' caught your eye, and you picked it up."

Why had Wakasako selected that title?

I was certain the book had whispered to him.

"You look like you don't have anywhere to go. How about taking shelter from the rain for a bit?"

I did not believe the book had any evil intentions.

After all, normal humans couldn't hear the voices of books. But Wakasako happened to be in exactly the same circumstances as the servant in "Rashōmon." Though he couldn't hear the invitation, his heart had sensed it, and he was enchanted by it.

"When you went to the library, you had lost your chance to become a manager and were depressed, right? You joined the orchestra club and immediately put in an honest effort to become the leader of the first-years, even winning the trust of the upperclassmen. Despite all that—a baseless, damaging rumor about your middle school days cost you everyone's support. You were worried all your hard work had gone to waste again, weren't you? You weren't sure what you were going to do next. Your future looked dark as night."

"I don't know! I don't know!" Wakasako shouted down at us, still clinging to the water tower ladder. "I don't know! I don't know!"

Haruto placed a hand on the ladder and was about to climb up, but I urged to him to wait, then resumed speaking.

"The servant in 'Rashōmon' feels the same way as you, Wakasako. He's been dismissed by the master he served for many years and has no idea how he will live through the next day. With no place to go, he takes shelter under the Rashōmon gate, driven there by the rain, at a loss for what to do."

In the capital city where the servant lives, natural disasters including an earthquake, a whirlwind, fires, and famine have compounded on one another, leading to total decline. The Rashōmon gate houses foxes, thieves, and even unclaimed corpses that have been abandoned. With an eye toward those corpses, a murder of crows flies in a circle over the gate at sunset.

In this wretched place, the servant agonizes over his options. He no longer has the privilege of relying on moral means to get through his hopeless situation.

"The servant deliberates over whether to lower himself to thievery, but he wavers in the face of a firm decision. If he is resolved to live, he is certain a life of crime can't be avoided. But he hesitates to actively make that vision a reality and can't work up the courage to commit evil acts."

Shaking the ladder, Wakasako groaned. "Uuurgh, evil— I can't be evil…! Dishonesty is unacceptable! I mustn't become like the rabble!" His voice shook.

Wakasako knew that the upperclassmen who had backed his rival candidate had spread the false rumor and spurred his fall. It must have been too late whenever he'd realized it, and by then, he had already lost everything to the antagonists who had perpetrated the wrongdoing.

Doing the right thing hadn't helped him at all.

In fact, he had lost everything.

In that case, wasn't stooping to their level the next best thing? Conduct himself a bit more cunningly and do whatever it took, no matter how dishonest—surely he must have grappled with the idea and been consumed by inner conflict.

Because he's such an upstanding guy.

"The servant, hoping to find a place where he can shelter from the driving rain and sleep for the night, climbs up the stairs in one of the pillars to get to the top floor of the Rashōmon gatehouse. But something prevents him from finishing the climb, doesn't it? At the top of the staircase, terrible things lie in wait, the likes of which the servant has never seen or experienced before. If he can push through despite his fear, he will know he has the makings of a rogue in him. He must be holding out that hope as he climbs!"

If he doesn't become a thief, he will starve and die in the gutter like a dog.

Yet he can't commit to evil.

Just like how Wakasako had regretted doing the right thing and flirted with the idea of becoming immoral but couldn't commit to a decision.

The servant, too, has sought higher ground, while worrying over a huge pimple that has formed on his right cheek.

Wakasako and the servant from the story shared the same feelings, and on that day, "Rashōmon" had called out to him. He had picked up the anthology and resonated with the servant's indecision and been infected by it. I was certain he had started repeatedly touching his right cheek because he felt as though a pimple had sprouted there.

"In the room at the top of the Rashōmon gatehouse, countless bodies have been callously discarded, and the stench of their decomposition hangs in the air. An emaciated old woman with a shock of white hair traipses among the bodies, plucking long hairs from the head of a female corpse one by one like a grooming monkey. The moment he beholds the old woman, the servant realizes the unforgivable evil of her actions and abandons his plan to become a thief. He is filled with hatred for the woman. He probably feels so indignant about her actions because he, too, has been debating whether to go down the path of evil."

Surely the woman's actions repulse the servant. He must find her detestable, this old woman so calmly committing an act of desecration.

Many readers could not decipher what was going on in the servant's heart, but to others, it was all too clear.

Wakasako also surely—

"Wakasako, you understand why the servant detests the old woman, right? After all, when the upperclassmen of the orchestra club committed a minor offense right before your eyes, as if it was only natural, your mind went blank with anger. You couldn't accept their actions, right?"

He shook the ladder hard.

"I was—just angry! But—do you think I could stand to be lumped in with such foul company? Dishonesty is wrong, no matter if everyone is doing it. The more you deny the truth, the more you'll lose your way and the more you'll suffer, right?"

And now he, too, was suffering.

"The servant points his sword at the old woman and demands to know what she is doing there," I continued. "Her answer is mundane—that she is planning to take the hair and make wigs. The servant despairs, and at the same time, a new kind of loathing wells up inside him alongside icy scorn. But the old woman counters the servant. 'What I am doing is not evil. If I don't do this, I'll starve to death. I don't have any other option,' she says."

"This is just normal stuff! Everyone does it, geez."

That's how the upperclassmen answered an underclassman who had challenged their actions.

Those words flipped a dangerous switch in Wakasako, who was by that time infected by "Rashōmon."

The old woman in the story insists that she cannot help but commit an evil act.

The upperclassmen had insisted that what they were doing was okay because everyone did it.

"When the servant hears the old woman's words, he takes the hand covering his pimple off his cheek and says, 'Well then, you won't begrudge me if I take your clothes. If I don't do that, I'll starve to death.' —Then he strips the old woman of her kimono, dashes back down the ladder, and disappears into the night.

"The old woman crawls to the top of the ladder, sticks her head out of the opening upside down, and peers out at the space beneath the gate but sees only pitch-black night outside.

"'What happened to the lowly servant, no one knows.' So it is written, and so the story ends."

* * *

"Saw everything...upside down."

That's where Princess Yonaga's words had pointed.

The old woman, who sticks her head out upside down from the top story of the gatehouse.

Reversal of good and evil.

"When the upperclassmen told Wakasako that everyone did what they were doing and so it was nothing to worry about, his feelings and the feelings of the servant in the story aligned. That's why he ripped off that guy's clothes and ran off with them—"

Overhead, an animalistic scream rang out.

Wakasako was twisting his body around in anguish.

"Raaahhhhh! Aaaarghhh! Aaaaaaaahhhh!"

"Shit, Musubu, he's lost control of himself! If he loses his grip in that position and falls, he'll be seriously injured!"

"Wait, just a little more—" Sweat beaded on my forehead and my head rang like an alarm bell as I held Haruto back. My mind flashed back to the bloodred sky and the piled-up bodies, the images flickering across my vision. The smell of decay clung to the inside of my nose, making me nauseated.

The bodies! The rotting bodies! The heap of bodies! The bodies crawling with maggots! The stinking bodies—

"Aaaaaaah! I'll be eaten! By the darkness—by the night—I'll be swallowed up! Aaaaaaah!"

Wakasako's screams sounded just like my own—

"Musubu...Musubu...don't get too entranced. If you let yourself be drawn in by any book other than me, I'll curse you. I'm a hundred times more brutal and fearful and charming, aren't I?"

I almost fell under the story's influence, but Princess Yonaga's desperate, cherubic voice broke the spell. Surely that was why she had asked me to bring her with me.

So that she could bring me back to myself.

Thank you, Princess Yonaga. It's because of you that I can hold my ground.

Something landed heavily on my head.

It was the uniform Wakasako had been holding at his side. He let go of the ladder with one hand and hung his head, pressing that hand to his right cheek while violently writhing.

"Watch out, Wakasako!" Haruto called.

But he didn't seem to hear his warning. He was single-mindedly chanting the phrases "I'll be eaten. I'll be swallowed up."

The servant, who strips the kimono from the old woman.

Wakasako, who had seized the shirt and jacket from the orchestra club upperclassman.

Both of them had crossed a line after vacillating between good and evil and had ultimately chosen evil, then disappeared into the darkness.

Where they went, no one knew.

"I don't know."

"I don't know."

"I don't know, I don't know, I don't know."

Princess Yonaga's words.

The chorus of books in the library.

"I don't know."

"What happened to the lowly servant, no one knows."

Wakasako must have feared that once he finished reading the final line, he would be swallowed up by the cold darkness and plummet into an endless abyss.

In that case, there was something I had to communicate to him.

* * *

"Wakasako! What do you think is the best part of 'Rashōmon'?"

I shouted my question loudly as he trembled with his right hand pressed against his cheek, muttering something about fearing the darkness would devour him.

"Is it that it's a brief and dispassionate story?" I asked.

"Or is it the vacillation of the servant?"

"Or perhaps it's the ultimate reversal of good and evil?"

A boy who could hear the voices of books, and a boy who was being possessed by one. I faced Wakasako and revealed to him the true nature of the book imbued with the spirit of the great genius Ryūnosuke Akutagawa!

"Ah, all these things are incredible! In the course of such a brief story, the reader is surprised, conflicted, and drawn into the story again and again. Just as you would expect from a bestseller that's been read continuously for a hundred years! But what elevates this work to an eternal masterpiece is that last line!"

The sky had completely darkened, and the damp breeze had chilled. Wakasako had stopped screaming and now merely trembled. His right hand clutched his cheek again.

"'What happened to the lowly servant, no one knows.' —Thanks to this single sentence, 'Rashōmon' achieved immortal brilliance. What thoughts stirred in you when you read that final line, Wakasako? How did you feel?"

My words, the ambiguity of the final line, and the overwhelming fear he felt—they all must have flashed vividly into his mind and triggered something. He howled like a beast again.

"Aaaaaaaah!"

"That's right—after you shuddered in horror, you were filled with fear. You imagined that the servant, who chooses evil, being swallowed up by

the endless darkness and falling into the eternal pit of hell, didn't you? And you believed that you, too, were destined for that same fate and would fall ever lower. You were scared, scared, scared, so scared you couldn't stand it, right?"

"Scared… That's right, I was scared…scared…"

Wakasako leaned his head against the ladder and sobbed. He had put in the effort, tried his best, bravely faced many setbacks—but the second defeat was too much.

It must have seemed as though, no matter how hard he tried, he would only end up losing like this again. He had nowhere left to go. His destination was unclear.

"Wakasako, I still remember the miserable look on your face as you told me you had no future. In your mind, the future of the servant from 'Rashōmon' disappears with him into the darkness, cut off from the world. But you know what? The author, Ryūnosuke Akutagawa, rewrote that final sentence several times."

Up in the darkness, I saw Wakasako hunched over and sobbing frailly.

That's right—Akutagawa himself was also going through a great trial in the darkness. Searching for a way to fix "Rashōmon" in the minds of his readers for all eternity. Seeking the perfect ending.

"In the magazine *Teikoku Bungaku*, where 'Rashōmon' first appeared, that final line was 'The servant had already braved the rain and headed off into the city of Kyoto to begin working as a thief.' In Akutagawa's first collection of short stories, it became 'The servant had already braved the rain and headed off into the city of Kyoto, having begun his work as a thief.' And then, in Taisho 7, 1918, two and a half years after the story was first published, it was reprinted in the anthology with 'The Nose,' finally with its current last line."

"What happened to the lowly servant, no one knows."

"Why did he keep rewriting the final line like this? I think it was because Akutagawa kept on ruminating over this story, because the servant, unstable and adrift in worry and conflict, was a part of Akutagawa himself. And so literary master Ryūnosuke Akutagawa settled at last on the supreme sentence for all his readers: 'No one knows'!"

Wakasako's right hand still guarded his right cheek. His shoulders and limbs still quivered. But I was sure it would only be a little longer.

He had always rejected the idea of turning to dishonesty, so when he actually did something wrong, it frightened him and made him feel he would be swallowed up by darkness.

But those who are truly evil view the darkness as an ally that hides their misdeeds. Wakasako, who feared the dark, was still a good person at heart.

"When you read that final line, Wakasako, you probably felt as if there was a deep blackness spreading out before you. But me? —When I read it, I felt liberated."

His shoulders hitched up in surprise, and then his shaking stopped.

He's probably puzzled right now, wondering how I could find liberation in a chilling sentence that gave him nothing but dread.

"Do you think I'm lying? It's the truth. To me, 'Rashōmon' is the story of a lone man who, despite losing his job, having no place to go, and thinking he has no choice but to turn to evil, can't find the will to embark on a life of crime. So he climbs the gate and in doing so is released from all that conflict. What happens to him after he disappears into the darkness? I'm convinced he lives boldly and freely. He probably takes up the life of a thief, crosses that dangerous bridge easily, strikes it rich, then lives a carefree existence. Maybe he rises in the world from a bandit to a high-ranking samurai—whenever I read that last line, I can't help but come up with something romantic. To me, that is the exhilaration of 'Rashōmon.'"

What happened to the lowly servant, no one knew.

It is precisely because no one knows that the reader holding the book can imagine his fate freely.

The servant has an infinite number of futures, limited only by the number of readers. His path spreads out unendingly before him.

I kept on speaking to Wakasako, who still had his back turned to me in a bewildered sort of silence.

"Even if everyone reads the same story, they'll feel differently about it and come up with their own interpretation. In fact, that happens even with the same reader. A story hits you differently depending on whether you read it when you're sad or happy or worried. That's why I can't help but read the same thing over and over again. Wakasako, try reading 'Rashōmon' again! No, three times, or four times, or as many times as you want! I'm certain you'll see a different future every time you do."

Your future is not lost.

I can see the light of the morning sun rising just beyond the darkness.

Gradually, bit by bit, the hand that held Wakasako's right cheek lowered.

I want you to realize there's no pimple there.

I want you to realize you are the only one who can determine your future.

"The servant who lacks the conviction to become immoral climbs the Rashōmon gatehouse hoping to change something about his situation. The moment he decides to climb up those steps—the moment he decides he wants to change—the servant himself has already done so. Wakasako, you're the same way! You read 'Rashōmon' and felt conflicted, and in that moment, you changed! You are free to choose between good and evil! That's right! You were liberated, set loose! That's nothing to be afraid of! Your futures are infinite and innumerable! Like the servant, who dashes off without hesitation into the darkness, your legend is just beginning!"

Mixed in with the chorus of books chanting **"I don't know"** in the library, there had been one aged voice, heavy and profound.

"Do as you please."

I see—that must have been the voice of "Rashōmon" itself.

Yes, it had infected a troubled high school boy, but it had been worried about him, so it had offered some advice. *Decide your own future however you like*, it had suggested.

Wakasako's right hand hung limply from his arm.

Haruto grabbed on to the ladder in a panic, but Wakasako didn't fall off. He regained a tight grip on the ladder with both hands now that they were free, but instead of climbing down, he headed up.

That's right—up.

Up and up.

He grew steadily closer to the indigo sky that was beginning to twinkle brightly with stars.

"Do as you please."

"Your true future is the one you choose."

The voice of "Rashōmon" surely echoed in the depths of Wakasako's ears. Even if he couldn't hear it, he could feel it.

With powerful steps, he ascended the ladder rung by rung.

When he finally reached the top of the water tower, he spread his legs and struck a monumental pose. The figure of Wakasako seemed free, seemed larger than life. He stretched both hands up high toward the heavens—and laughed.

"This is the first time I've ever been so high up! Ah-ha-ha, the sky is so close. I feel like I could grab the stars. It feels so good!"

He sounded as if he was slipping free of the past. Then he laughed and laughed. We watched him from the base of the water tower, and when he looked down at us, his eyes were as bright and sparkling as the stars.

Wakasako turned and spoke to me like a friend. "I get what you mean when you say 'Rashōmon' is a liberating story. That interpretation makes sense, too. Thank you, Enoki! I'm going to try reading 'Rashōmon' again! If I do that, maybe I'll be able to see a different story, just like you said."

"I was pretty nervous when Wakasako took his hand off the ladder, but you proved as reliable as ever, Musubu."

Three days later—

In the conference room of the music hall, Haruto was thanking me again. On the marble table, a three-tiered stand was stacked high with a glittering array of scones, sandwiches, bite-size cakes, chocolates, and more.

"I ran into Wakasako in the hall today, and he said hello. He looked well. How's he doing in orchestra club?"

Although he hadn't exactly been in control of himself, he did tear off an upperclassman's clothes and run away screaming, so I was worried about whether being in the club had become difficult for him.

"Ah, well, I can't say there's absolutely no trouble at all, but it seems like it'll be okay. I made public the fact that someone in the club had spread the rumors about Wakasako, so they reconsidered endorsing him for the manager position, but Wakasako turned it down. He said he still hopes to become club president in the end, though. Seems he's not giving up. He should be fun to have around from now on."

I saw Haruto smile, and I got excited, too.

Yep, looks like Wakasako's future is bright.

"By the way, Musubu, what did you plan to do if Wakasako had dashed down the path of evil once he was liberated from his moral dilemma?"

"That was always a possibility. Especially since the idea of what's good and what's evil is something that changes easily with time and circumstance. Besides, if evil completely vanished from the world, books would get pretty boring, huh?"

"I think you might be the most villainous person there is, Musubu."

"Huh? What's that supposed to mean?"

Haruto was unfazed as I stared at him from behind a scone covered in clotted cream.

Good grief, which one of us is evil again?

The next day, I went to say a few words to the "Rashōmon" in the library.

When I thanked it for the advice it had offered, it answered in a dignified voice.

"I know not what you mean."

And then, there was the indigo book that had held me in check up on the roof—

"Musubu...you're late. You don't love me enough."

She was waiting for me on my desk when I got home. In my mind, I saw the princess sitting properly, clad in a noble blue kimono, pouting and looking the other way. She had a cute voice.

"I'm sorry. Haruto called me to the music hall, and we talked for a while."

"Cheating with another book again?"

"That's not it! We were talking about how Wakasako seems to be doing well."

"Really? ...Was that all? Come on... I've told you that you mustn't accept requests from that character anymore."

She was adorable even when issuing warnings, and my face relaxed into a smile as I answered her.

"It's all right. Final exams are already over, so now I've got plenty of time to spend talking with you."

Her chilly voice was tinged with happiness. **"You do need to apologize for doing something perilous and making me fret, so...you'll be spending the entire break with me."**

Ah, my girlfriend is cute and carefree again today. Although, like Wakasako, I don't have any clear prospects for the future yet.

But as long as the cold, frightening, charming blue book was in my bag or my pocket, I was certain my future held clear skies.

Book 4

A Summer Running Wild with *Fifteen Boys*

"I wanna go on an adventure!"

In a lively, boyish voice, *he* insisted, "I want to drift away to a deserted island with no adults, where we dig out caves to make our homes, and fish and hunt for food, and gather shellfish and fruits to survive, and explore the interior of the island, and fly through the sky tied to kites, and fight bravely against villains of all sorts—I want to have a thrilling, heart-pumping adventure like that!"

That's exactly what's written in your story, you know, I thought as I listened to him. But that fact did little to dull his enthusiasm.

Summer vacation had just started, and here in the town library, a "recommended summer reading" section had been set up for students of all ages who needed to write book reports for homework. One of those books had started speaking to me. On its cover was an illustration of a group of boys holding things like spyglasses and muskets. Still glossy and bright, it must have been a recent acquisition.

The title on the cover read *The Story of Fifteen Boys.* It's an adventure story for boys written by the French author Jules Verne in the late nineteenth century, also known as *Two Years' Holiday.* The voice seemed to belong to an abridged version, written succinctly so that it would be easy for children to read.

Next to it sat a hardcover edition of *The Story of Fifteen Boys.* This version was quite old and was already missing its cover. Its pages were yellowed, and it was heavy and thick. Whether because it found the chatter of the fresh newcomer to be annoying, or it reckoned that young books couldn't help but gab, the old tome was silent.

The new copy passionately appealed to me. **"I may have happened to be born as a book, but the blood of an adventurer runs through me! I'm not meant to sit in a safe, air-conditioned room being read. Let's break our bindings and strike out on the sea! Hey, you with the glasses, you can hear my voice, can't you? Get me out of this place! Let's go on an adventure together!"**

I answered the book in my mind. *Sorry, I'm an indoor person.*

Then I stood up and left.

I thought that would be the end of it, but—

"Adventure on a deserted island? Sounds great!"

Later, when I told Haruto about meeting an unusual book, he leaned forward in excitement. "It's perfect timing—we're just starting summer vacation, and I happen to know of several deserted islands, so I'll ask around. I'll contact you with the dates later, but it would be great if you could go borrow that copy of *The Story of Fifteen Boys*, Musubu."

Huh? Wha—?

Deserted islands? Huh? Whaaat?!

Haruto told me he had some idea of what to do about lodgings and that I should leave everything up to him, or something like that. In any case, my participation seemed to be taken as a given.

I was still panicking when I got a message from Haruto later that day. In it, he told me an acquaintance of his owned a deserted island that he hadn't used since he bought it, and we were free to use it as we pleased.

My plan to spend summer vacation in an air-conditioned room, lost in my books, was no more—we would be shipping off to a deserted island.

Three days later—

I clung desperately to the rail of a boat being tossed about by violent waves and pelted by rain that fell like stones.

"Why did we have to choose a day like this to leeeave?" I whined. "And why did we transfer to this tiny boooat?"

When we left the port in the Himekura family's large yacht, I had felt relatively safe, figuring a little rain and wind would be no problem in such a fancy vessel. The cabin inside was comfortable, with fluffy couches and everything, and I didn't even feel seasick.

And then, once night fell and the rain started coming down harder—

"Okay, from here on, it's just us guys going."

Haruto had insisted we make our own way to the deserted island in a tiny boat—one that didn't even have a roof—being thrashed by the waves. The only saving grace was that we didn't have to row ourselves with oars.

The Campus Prince himself served as our driver. "I got my small-boat license last month!" he told me.

So you're basically a beginner!

Wait, can high schoolers even get boating licenses?

"Whoa! The waves! There's water in the boooat!"

"Calm down, Enoki. Toss it back out with the bucket."

One of the underclassmen in the orchestra club, a first-year student like me named Wakasako, whom Haruto had somehow roped into our outrageous outing, handed me a bucket. He remained calm even as the boat was tossed about to the point that we were taking on water, and he briskly set about scooping up water in the bucket before tossing it back into the sea.

"Our mast has broken, but she's still sailing along with no dip in speed, so leave it to me." Haruto spoke as if he were a character in *The Story of Fifteen Boys.*

"We never had a mast to begin with!"

"Enoki, watch out! A wave's coming from behind! Hold on tight!"

"Don't you start playing make-believe, too, Wakasako— Ah, you weren't kidding!"

When I turned around to look, all I could see was a massive wave bearing down on us like a huge black bear with both arms spread wide. The water came crashing over me, flooding my nose and mouth with salty brine and making my head spin as if I had just been sucker punched.

With the inside of the boat inundated, I was sure we'd be done for if another wave like that came over—we'd definitely sink. Fighting my fears, I desperately scooped up water in my bucket and heaved it over the side.

A delighted voice rose from my jacket pocket.

"That wave was amaaazing! This is what I was talking about, this right here! You can't experience this in a box at the library. This is the thrill and adventure I've always wanted!"

Wrapped snugly in waterproof plastic, *The Story of Fifteen Boys*, or Fifteen for short, was in high spirits.

"This is about the point when Moko gets himself entwined in rope and is about to be strangled to death, before Briant finds him and cuts the rope with a knife to save him. Musubu! Do you think you could get a rope out of the luggage and wrap yourself up in it?"

I was starting to consider throwing Fifteen overboard. But another wave was bearing down on us, and I was working feverishly to bail out the water with my bucket.

"Ahhhhh!" I shouted. "I don't want to end up in the newspaper—'Three High School Boys Capsize and Die, Boating on a Stormy Night!' Aaaahhh!"

"You'll be fine! Go, go, go!"

Don't tell me to "go, go, go," you!

"I really, really thought we were gonna die back there."

The three of us sat on the beach in a daze, having finally reached solid land.

"Distance-wise, it's actually not far to this deserted island," Haruto mused, "but Musubu was acting way too scared, so I took us for a few spins around the island for his sake." He grinned devilishly. "I'm pleased to see I got you to enjoy the 'shipwrecked in a stormy sea' section of our adventure."

Are you kidding me? Who would ever enjoy that?!

Unlike me, Wakasako had kept his composure. He was busy pulling all our luggage off the boat.

"Where are we going to set up camp?" he asked Haruto. "We've got plastic sheets, so we should be able to put up some tents pretty easily."

"Tents, huh?" Haruto nodded. "I was planning to find a cave somewhere, but that works, too."

"All right, I'm going to get water from the river," Wakasako said. "Let's boil it before we use it. Before that, we need to gather tree branches and build a fire…"

"You sure know your stuff. Have you been stranded on a deserted island before?" Haruto asked.

"Yeah, right!" Wakasako shrugged. "I was in the Boy Scouts in elementary and middle school, and we went camping every year, so I'm used to it, is all."

"Oh really, that'll come in handy!"

Wakasako beamed at Haruto's praise. If Haruto was the main character Briant, with his heroics and leadership, maybe Wakasako was the calm, cool, and collected Gordon? No, maybe he was the devoted and eminently capable sailor's apprentice Moko? For the time being, I seemed to have been pressed into the service of a couple of adventure maniacs.

"All right, we'll leave pitching the tents to Wakasako—Musubu, you help him. I'm going to go procure some food."

I nearly leaped as Haruto pulled a rifle from his luggage.

"Wait! That's a violation of the Firearm and Sword Possession Control Law!"

"Worry not. I regularly go shooting at foreign gun ranges, so I'm confident in my skills. Didn't you know, Musubu? In America, you can even buy guns in children's sizes!"

This is Japan! I nearly exclaimed. But then I stopped myself. Were we even in Japan anymore? From inside my pocket, Fifteen hassled me as I puzzled it over.

"All riiight! Let's hunt up plenty of game! Tonight we eat rabbit stew!"

"No, stop it! Briant and the other characters from the book may hunt with guns, but we can't! Even if you shoot a bird or rabbit or something, we can't clean it! Just thinking about tearing out feathers or fur or whatever…

Aaahhh!" I gripped my shoulders with both arms and trembled. "I just can't do it! If you have to go catch something, catch fish!"

"But we came all this way to a deserted island… Besides, I didn't bring a fishing pole." Haruto looked at his rifle regretfully.

Wakasako offered a helping hand. "We can make the rod and hooks from tree branches or vines. For the line, we should be able to unravel some rope to get thin strands. I'll make it."

"Wow, really? In that case, I want to try making one myself," Haruto said. "Would you teach me how?"

"Sure thing. I think we should also be able to set traps in the river."

"Great! Show me how to do that, too."

I breathed a sigh of relief once Haruto's interest turned away from hunting.

"Awww, we're not going hunting? I wanted to eat roast duck! The kind dripping with fat!"

Fifteen was making a fuss, but he couldn't even eat anything anyway.

And that is how our life on a deserted island began.

While Haruto went to fish using the pole Wakasako had helped him make, Wakasako and I put up the tents, gathered wood, and built a hearth.

Perhaps "Wakasako and I" was generous—he did about ten times as much work as I did.

He really is like Moko, isn't he…?

"It's a good thing you're here with us, Wakasako," I said. "If it was just me and Haruto, he probably would have gone shooting, and I'd be sitting here plucking out rabbit fur and crying. But you really got on board with the plan to play *The Story of Fifteen Boys* on a deserted island, huh? Though I'm not much use."

"You weren't excited about coming, Enoki?"

"I've always been more of an indoor kind of guy."

"Oh really? But Haruto told me this was your idea."

"My idea…? When I was talking about *The Story of Fifteen Boys*, Haruto said it sounded fun, and everything snowballed from there."

"Ah, right. You told me you and Haruto are book buddies."

"Mm, sort of."

Wakasako didn't know I could speak to books. But he was very grateful to me after the "Rashōmon" incident, and we had gotten along ever since.

"I'm sure Haruto reached out to me because he was thinking of my standing in the orchestra club. I caused that whole mess right before summer break, so even now a lot of people in the club see me as 'the psycho who snapped and tore off an upperclassman's clothes before running away yelling.' I think that as the leader of the orchestra club, Haruto took the initiative to invite me on a personal holiday as a way of showing everyone that he still believes in me."

Thanks to Haruto's efforts, nobody trash-talked Wakasako anymore, at least not in the open. He told me he was grateful for everything Haruto had done for him.

"Haruto isn't just the chairwoman's son. He's also a natural leader. That must be why everyone always follows Haruto's lead."

It seemed Wakasako had a great deal of confidence in Haruto.

Just as I suspected, Wakasako isn't Gordon—he's Moko.

By the time Haruto returned to camp, we had finished pitching the tents and building the hearth and had started a huge fire going to boil our water.

"Look at all this fish!"

Haruto was exuberant as he presented us the fish overflowing in his bucket. Back in the music hall, Haruto had always played the part of an elegant prince who carried himself with the grace befitting his noble lineage. But now, with the sleeves of his half-soaked shirt rolled up to his elbows and bare feet beneath his shorts, carrying a handmade fishing pole and a bucket while guffawing with his mouth open wide, he was the spitting image of a mischievous little grade schooler.

"Wow, amazing! There are so many!"

"Big catch! It's a big catch!"

Fifteen was also in high spirits.

"I wanna go fishing, too! I wanna catch a fish!"

Sure, okay, next time.

"Wakasako, I want to skewer and roast these. What's the best way to do it?" Haruto asked.

"First we have to take out the guts. If we've got disposable chopsticks, those are good, but we could also use twigs as a substitute. Put the sticks in through the mouth and twist them around and around to try to wind the innards up," Wakasako instructed.

"All right, let's give it a try. How about it, Musubu?"

"Uh, I'm a little uneasy when it comes to innards...," I replied. "I'm an indoor kind of guy, so—"

"Aw, don't say that. We came all the way out to a deserted island. Here." Haruto found a good-looking twig and handed it to me.

Fifteen was making a racket in my pocket. **"Let's do it! Twist up the guts!"**

Ewww... W-well, I guess it's still better than having to pull out rabbit fur?

Suddenly, I shrieked. "Um, my fish is alive! It's still alive!"

"Yeah, they're so fresh, they're still jumping!"

Haruto grabbed a fish and thrust his stick in through its mouth.

"Eeeeeep!"

"Oh, Haruto? It's easier to twirl everything up if you put two sticks in and move them at the same time. Here."

"Thanks, Wakasako." Haruto took the second stick from Wakasako and thrust it right in!

"Gaaaaaah!"

"What's wrong now, Musubu?"

I should be the one asking you—how can you do that without any hesitation? Twisting sticks and pulling out guts like it's nothiiiiing?!

"All right, we're getting them out pretty well. Hey, you try, too, Musubu."

"Twist and turn! Faster, faster!"

"Uuugh."

Whenever I grabbed one of the frantically thrashing fish from the bucket with my bare hand, the slimy texture gave me goose bumps.

"Ew, ew, ew!"

Halfway in tears, I inserted my two sticks into the fish's mouth as it tried to escape. As I twisted them around, the fish gradually stopped moving. Then, I wrenched the bloody, mixed-up innards from the fish, along with an awful stench, screaming all the while.

"Augh!"

"Wow!"

"Hyahhh!"

"You got a lot out!"

"Gyehhh!"

"Musubu, do that big one next!"

Fifteen sounded as if he was having the time of his life in my pocket.

This is the last time I eat fish...

Or so I thought, but by the time we got the innards out, skewered the fish on sticks made from tree branches, sprinkled them with salt from the boat, and stuck them upright around the campfire to start roasting them, the appetizing aroma drifting up around us, my stomach was growling.

Ah...somehow it smells good.

Wow, the skin is all crispy and looks delicious.

And the fat is dripping down... Mmm.

"All right, that should be about good. They're hot, so be careful, Enoki."

Wakasako handed me one of the piping-hot fish. Haruto had already sunk his teeth into the biggest, most tender one, starting from the head.

"This is the greatest!" he raved. "It's even better than what you get at one of those Michelin star restaurants."

I couldn't resist the mouthwatering aroma that wafted up from the skewer in my hands, and I bit into the middle of the fish.

"Whoa!"

"What is it, Musubu?"

"Enoki, was there a stone or something in yours?"

"Is it a poisonous fish?!"

Trembling, I groaned, "...Damn, it's so good."

"Told you."

"Don't scare us like that!"

"Me too, I want to eat some, too!"

The atmosphere around the campfire had turned as warm as the flaky fish.

The rice porridge with mushrooms, herbs, and canned beans that Wakasako had prepared for us was equally delicious, and we all ate ravenously.

Once the sun had set and night had fallen, the stars sparkled brightly across the whole sky.

"Wow...when people write about night skies that look like they're strewn with diamonds, this must be what they mean."

Lying by our bonfire on the beach, we looked up at the sky with wide eyes.

You can't see these kinds of stars in the city.

Wakasako pointed his finger upward and identified a few constellations. "That one's Lyra, the one over there's Aquila, and that far one is Cygnus."

"Lyra, Aquila, and Cygnus, wow!" Fifteen listened in rapture.

Haruto seemed to be enjoying himself as well. "I've got a proposal," he announced. "If we're going to live here together, we need a leader, right? How about we decide on a president?" he suggested.

I suppose he wanted to do it because there was a scene in *The Story of Fifteen Boys* where they choose a president, but in that book, there are fifteen of them, whereas we counted only three among our ranks. Really, there was no need to choose a president, as Haruto had already naturally assumed a leadership role as the oldest.

What's the point of even bothering with an election? Hang on, I think he just wants to have someone call him "President."

I had my jokes all lined up, but Wakasako happily went along with Haruto's suggestion. "Sure. Should we put it to a vote?"

Fifteen revved up again from inside my pocket. **"A president!"**

Well, okay then.

We decided to hold the vote by putting our marks on a rock—a vote for Haruto would be one line, a vote for Wakasako was two lines, and a vote for me was three.

"Me too! Me too!"

Fifteen was adamant, but I calmed him down. "You'll sit this one out," I told him and put my stone in the bucket.

Once everyone had put his stone in (there were only three of us, mind you), we counted.

The result was one stone with one line, one stone with two lines, and one stone with three lines...

Uh-oh…

We stared down at the three stones for a while.

Haruto snickered. "A complete tie, huh?"

"Should we redo it?" I asked.

"Nah, we'll all be president. Doesn't that sound nice?"

"That sounds good, too."

Fifteen was delighted to hear this.

"Does that mean I'm president, too? Hooray!"

And that's how our first day drew to a close.

On days two and three, we continued living as castaways. We hunted for food and explored the island, made rafts and floated around on the water, dived into the ocean and felt deeply moved by the blue of the sky when we looked up at it from the sea, and played Tarzan by swinging between trees on vines.

Being an indoor type, I had already had enough adventures to last me a whole year—I was completely and utterly exhausted. But washing my face in the river water first thing in the morning did feel nice, and I got pretty used to taking the guts out of fish. The smoked meat, shellfish soups, and herb-roasted fish that Wakasako made for us were all scrumptious.

Then, on the fourth day—I awoke when it was still dark out and found Haruto missing.

Putting on my glasses as I left the tent, I saw him down at the beach, sitting with his arms around his knees and looking out at the ocean.

A handsome guy staring out into the ocean… *If a girl walked by, she'd take one look and fall in love. But somehow the mood seems somber…*

"What're you doing?"

Haruto turned and smiled. "I wanted to see the morning sun rise over the horizon."

"I see."

"Stay and watch it with me since you're up, Musubu."

"Well, all right."

I sat down next to him.

If you'd told me a year ago that I'd end up sitting beside the Campus Prince on a deserted island while watching the sunrise…I'd never have believed you…

Though books may have brought us together, there were still times when my discussions with Haruto didn't feel quite real. I often wondered how I was able to converse so freely with him.

From beside me, Haruto mumbled, "…There was a time when I didn't talk to anyone, you know."

When I turned to look at him, I saw that a dark shadow had fallen over his graceful features. I was shocked.

What happened? Why the sudden change?

"Musubu…what I did…you'd probably forgive me for it, but…I don't know about everyone else…"

What on earth could he have done to be murmuring so timidly and burying his face in his knees?! Don't tell me he shot someone with that rifle of his? Or is it some far more unspeakable crime that an ordinary person like me couldn't even begin to fathom…?

"Haruto, no matter what's weighing on you, talk to me. Please. I'll help you the best I can."

"…I was the one who untied the ropes on the boat."

"Huh?"

The ropes on the boat?

"Of course you're the one who untied them. I was right there. You said, 'All right, we're taking this boat the rest of the way!' so— Wait, are you doing an impression of Jack?!"

I recalled a scene in the book where Briant's little brother, Jack, confesses to a crime he had buried in his heart.

"Oh, you figured it out?"

"I did! Though you had me going for a second. I was worried, like a dummy."

"Sorry, sorry. I just couldn't resist." He lifted his face from his knees and laughed.

"Haruto, you've really been having a good time since we came here, haven't you? You know, I always thought of you as very grown-up, but now I think I see you in a different light."

"Ha-ha...I'm just having fun," Haruto said. But then his voice took on a twinge of loneliness. "It's because when you see me at school, I have to act like a Himekura and live up to my family name. Imagine the commotion if I ran around barefoot, frolicking and shouting about a big catch of fish, right?"

Well, yeah, it would be a surprise to see you catching fish at school or hear the slapping of your bare feet as you walked down the corridors, but...

That was a rather silly example, but still... I'd always figured Haruto could do whatever he wanted at school, but now his tone and expression both told me that wasn't exactly the case.

His name was well-known around campus, and all eyes were on him no matter where he went or what he did. He carried the weight of everyone's expectations. I'm sure it was far beyond what a four-eyed nobody like me could understand.

"That's why it's so fun for me to spend time here with you guys like this."

Haruto was enthusiastic about the trip right from the start. He must be under a lot of stress. I bet he'll dodge the question if I ask him about it, though. I'm just glad he's able let off some steam.

"I'm also having more fun than I thought," I admitted.

Haruto's lips curled into a smile. "Mm, knew you would."

"By the way, you voted for me in the presidential election, didn't you, Haruto?" I asked. "Why did you do that?"

"You caught me, huh?"

"Well, there's no way Wakasako was going to vote for anyone other than you."

"Which means you voted for Wakasako, right, Musubu? You thought he'd be a more fitting leader than me?"

"You're practically already a leader, so it would have been boring. And you voted for me because you thought it would spice things up somehow, was that it?"

"Yeah, I guess it was."

I knew it.

"But I know I can rely on you when it counts," he continued. "You saved my life, after all."

I felt a profound weight in my heart upon hearing those words. My expression turned solemn.

Indeed, Haruto and I had become acquainted through a terrifying and tragic incident.

I wonder where she is now. The girl who committed so many terrible crimes while under that book's spell. What could she be thinking at this very moment...?

I want to see...Princess Yonaga.

I recalled the slim book with the indigo cover that I had left back home—and I longed to see my coldly cute girlfriend.

She said not one word in parting after I told her I couldn't bring her along because life on a deserted island wouldn't suit a princess like her.

Whenever I so much as looked at another book, she would spew hatred and swear up and down that she would never pardon me for the act. She harbored a bottomless jealousy of other books, so the fact that I was taking a trip with one likely filled her heart with indignation.

"Absolutely unacceptable... I'll dance on your grave... I curse you. I'll chant my curses until the day you have eyes for no book but me."

As I imagined her sitting quietly and properly atop the lace handkerchief I had spread on my bed and muttering her curses, a jolt shot down my spine.

Ah, I've got to win back her favor somehow. Still, I'd prefer her to be angry instead of being sad that she's away from me...

"Musubu...I'm lonely. I want to see you..."

I pictured her shedding quiet tears from her innocent eyes and felt my chest tighten.

I want to see you, too.

I want to turn your pages...

With slight melancholy, I watched as the sun's rays unfolded like a fan from the horizon, and the world brightened before my eyes.

The incident happened on this day, the fourth day.

Around twilight, as I was returning from foraging for edible mushrooms and berries, the voice of a woman calling for help reached my ears.

"No, stop! Someone help!"

Approaching the source of the voice, I saw a man in a Hawaiian shirt and sunglasses digging a hole with a big shovel. I ducked into a nearby thicket to spy on him.

I thought we were supposed to be the only ones on this island!

"Come on, remember how you kept talking about how cute I am? Please think this through—I'm begging you!"

Beside the hole was a huge suitcase with wheels on it, from which a voice emanated.

Don't tell me there's a woman in there?!

The man, potbellied and about in his fifties, must have been tired from the work. He let out an enormous sigh. "Whew, time for a break."

Pulling the trunk along with him, he came to a boat beached on the sand and hauled the trunk on board.

Fifteen shouted from my pocket, **"Musubu, he's a bad guy—he's going to kill that lady! We have to help her!"**

Equally anxious to help, I rushed back to Haruto and Wakasako and reported what I had seen.

"There's a woman locked up in a trunk, and I think she's going to be buried alive!"

Wakasako stared at me, dumbstruck.

Haruto frowned and confirmed what I had told him. "You say the person digging the hole was a fifty-something man in a Hawaiian shirt and sunglasses, with a potbelly? Was there anyone else around?"

I shook my head. "Uh-uh, there was no one on the beach. But there might be others on the yacht."

"What should we do, Haruto?" asked Wakasako.

After thinking for a few moments, Haruto grew serious. "Let's fly a kite."

"Huh?"

There is a scene in *The Story of Fifteen Boys* where the boys fly a huge kite in order to identify the whereabouts of some villains who had docked on the island.

Briant soars through the air, riding in a fishing basket attached to the kite, and spies down on the surface from above with his telescope.

The kite is named Giant of the Skies.

"I thought something like this might happen if we were doing *The Story of Fifteen Boys*," Haruto said, "so I brought this with us. I'm glad it'll come in handy."

A very large piece of luggage that had been stacked up in the boat turned out to be a collapsible kite. It was big enough that a person could fasten it to their back and fly, and it had a long rope attached.

"This isn't good at all," I said. "Do we really need to fly a kite since we already know the location of the aloha man? Shouldn't we call the police like normal people or sneak over there and watch what he does or something?"

Haruto quickly rejected my insistence to take more appropriate measures. "If we wait for the police, the woman might die. Plus, there's nowhere to hide on the sand, so waltzing over there would be risky. It'll be night soon, so if we're in the air, he shouldn't notice us."

"No, he'll absolutely notice! This plan's got so many holes in it!"

I refused to back down, but Wakasako merely shrugged. "If that's what Haruto wants to do."

Fifteen immediately volunteered. **"I'll ride in the basket!"**

"Majority rules, two to one," Haruto nodded. "We're doing it. We'll be counting on you, Musubu."

"Wait, you want me to go up?"

"You're the lightest one among us, right?"

"That's right."

"Don't you agree with him, too, Wakasako!"

"Let's go! Musubu! I'll go with you!"

You be quiet!

"This is a job for the main character, Briant, right?! At best, I'm Briant's little brother, Jack, so it can't be me!" I insisted.

In the book, Jack insists on riding the kite himself to atone for his earlier crime, but Briant steps in.

"No, Jack, I'm the one who'll ride on it.

"As your older brother, I can atone for your crimes. Ever since I came up with this plan, I intended to be the one who goes up."

It's a breathtaking scene, befitting a main character.

"Listen, even Briant says he'll go up in the kite, since he's the one who thought up the plan! If you want to do this no matter what, you go right ahead, Haruto. It was *your* idea!"

He plunked his hands down on both my shoulders and addressed me with utmost confidence: "I think you're the only Briant here, Musubu. Now, let's hurry up and get everything ready."

I whined and wheedled, but neither of them listened. The two of them lashed the kite to my back, and when it caught a breeze, it lifted my short, slight body off the ground and into the night sky.

"Go, go! Giant of the Skies!" Fifteen shouted with great excitement from my pocket.

"Aaaaghhh!! It's high! So high!"

Haruto's voice came through the speaker of the smartphone I had in my other pocket. "Musubu, how is it? See anything?"

"I can't foooocus!"

In the book, the basket wobbles a lot at first, but after that, Briant feels no sense of danger. Conversely, because the kite was attached directly to my back, the wind tossed me about and sent the kite careening left and right, totally unstable.

I was in no mood to pretend I was in some fairy-tale land riding the back of a mysterious bird. My heart felt as if it were about to leap out of my mouth as I pondered when I would go crashing down.

Hoping to return to solid ground as quickly as possible, I peered desperately through the telescope I had taken up with me.

The yacht I had seen earlier that evening was anchored on the exact opposite shore from where we had set up our tents.

The man in the Hawaiian shirt emerged from the boat, schlepping the wheeled suitcase. Since night had fallen, he no longer wore sunglasses. His eyes were sharp, and his whole appearance was intimidating.

From this height, I couldn't hear anything below, but I wondered if the woman in the suitcase was all right.

The man went as far as the hole he had dug, then picked up the shovel and resumed his work.

I shouted at the smartphone, "The man came out just now and started digging the hole again!"

"Great, okay. Wakasako and I are headed that way. Musubu, you keep monitoring the situation."

"Huh? Waaaaaait, let me down already!"

But if the two of you head toward the man, won't that mean there will be nobody handling the rope keeping the kite in place?

How am I supposed to get down?!

"Musubu, let's go over there, too, and catch the bad guy!"

Fifteen made this courageous suggestion.

"We can't—we're stuck up here."

Just as I answered, a strong gust of wind buffeted the kite, and I pitched sideways.

"Ah! Augh! Wait!"

I tried to right myself, but struggling must have been the wrong thing to do, because I ended up tilted at even more of an angle. The kite began to spin.

"Aaaaahhhhh! S-stop this thiiiiiing!"

"Musubu, what happened?" Haruto asked.

"I'm falliiiiiing!"

It was too late. I had already begun my descent.

Fifteen shouted boldly, **"We're coming for you, bad guy!"**

My own screams drowned him out as I crash-landed, kite and all, onto the beach.

Sand obscured my glasses and covered my face, but perhaps because the kite had absorbed the impact of the fall, I seemed uninjured at the moment. I breathed a sigh of relief—then from nearby, I heard a rugged voice.

"Wh-who are you?!"

Through my sandy glasses, I could barely make out a fierce-looking man in a Hawaiian shirt who was holding a shovel in one hand and glaring at me.

"It's the bad guy!" Fifteen yelped.

Of all things, to crash right in front of him. I must have the worst luck in the world.

"Um, I'm, well, I was camping on the island, and..."

"Camping? This place is private property!"

Just then, I heard the voice from the suitcase again.

"Help me! I'll be buried alive!"

It's the woman's voice I heard earlier this evening!

"What do you have inside that suitcase?"

"What did you say?" The man's expression transformed before my eyes. After the initial alarm, he averted his gaze, as if hiding something shady. "Why would you ask that?"

"Because there's a woman's voice coming from it. She's begging for help."

"A...voice?" The man's gaze returned to me. He stared menacingly.

This was a real pinch.

"Musubu, go for it! Punch him!"

Fifteen was egging me on, but there was no way I was going to do that.

But, well—

"Please show me what's in the suitcase."

Musubu, you idiot! What'd you ask that for?!

"I can't do that." The man drew closer.

Aaaahhhh!

"Mr. Kusakabe."

I heard Haruto's voice. The man turned quickly in surprise.

Haruto and Wakasako strode into view.

They came!

But something is off here.

"Ha-Ha-*Haruto*, my boy! Why are you here?" the man asked, flustered.

Huh? Is he an acquaintance of Haruto's?

"I was doing some camping on the other side of the island with my friends. You didn't hear about it from your wife?"

"Uh, no, I… My wife doesn't really tell me these things, so…"

"Sorry for startling you," Haruto said. "Musubu, Wakasako, this is the island's owner, Mr. Kusakabe."

What the heck?! So the aloha man was the island's owner!

"By the way, Mr. Kusakabe, what are you doing here?" Haruto asked.

"Th-th-th-th-that's, well—"

"It looks like you've dug a hole, but what for?"

"The thing is, well, that's—"

"Do you think I could get you to open up that suitcase for me? Depending on what's in there, I might have to call the police, you see."

The agitated man's face immediately twisted in shock. "No, you can't! You can't! You can't! There's no way I can show you what's in here!"

"Help me!"

The voice again! Now it's certain!

I rushed over to the suitcase and undid the clasp. It wasn't locked, so the case immediately popped open. Inside, it was crammed full of girls in swimsuits, dozens and dozens of them—

…Wait, what?

* * *

"Help me! I don't want to be buried alive!"

"Come on, remember how you kept saying how cute I am?"

"You're going to throw us away? You're done with us? How cruel!"

The suitcase was full of photobooks depicting a popular young idol, including dozens of copies of one particular collection.

An idol with a pure and innocent image adorned the cover—even I had heard about her. Right before the start of summer break, she had announced she was pregnant and engaged to be married. It had been in the news every day since.

A number of boys in my class were even fans, and they had reacted to the news with lamentation, weeping sorrowfully over her photo collections.

"Dammit! Her fiancé is the president of an IT company! And she hid the fact that she was pregnant and stuff."

"I bet he had to buy a ton of CDs to win the chance to meet her."

The owner of the island, Mr. Kusakabe, shouted incoherently and tried to close the suitcase. But the lid refused to shut, and the photobooks kept spilling out. With the man too flustered to get the suitcase under control, things got increasingly out of hand.

"Th-th-th-th-this is…for work—"

"So you were a fan of Kokona Shimizu, Mr. Kusakabe?"

At Haruto's words, Mr. Kusakabe's face stiffened, and he turned toward us.

"I couldn't stand to put my carefully collected photobooks out for collection on garbage day, and I couldn't sell them off at the thrift shop, either. I thought coming all the way out here to a deserted island far from my house and burying them would be kind of romantic."

It seemed this Mr. Kusakabe had also been a fan of the popular idol. He had probably purchased multiple copies of CDs and photobooks in hopes of winning a chance to meet her. When her marriage was announced, he had apparently taken it just as hard as the boys in my class. So he decided to stop being her fan and dispose of her photobooks. But it would have been awfully embarrassing if anybody had caught him in the act, so he must have decided to sneak out to this deserted island that he happened to own, dig a deep hole, and bury them.

Despite his precautions, some high school boys and the firstborn son of a distinguished family had appeared out of nowhere on the ostensibly deserted island and discovered his embarrassing secret.

I was the one who had opened the suitcase, but now…I felt sort of sorry about it.

"H-H-H-H-Haruto, my boy! Please don't mention this to anyone—"

"My lips are sealed. I won't say a single word, not to your wife or your daughter, so please relax."

Haruto had deliberately invoked the man's wife and daughter. He had a mean streak.

Wakasako was silent, but one look at his face could tell you he was holding back some choice commentary.

"I'm c-counting on you, Haruto!"

As Mr. Kusakabe bowed repeatedly to a bunch of high schoolers, the photobooks in the suitcase stood up for him.

"Poor thing!"

"Sweet Kyosuke isn't a bad guy!"

"That's right—he let us live in a beautiful room and took good care of us!"

"Don't you bully our Kyosuke!"

They seemed to have forgotten they were about to be buried alive.

From inside my pocket, Fifteen burst with innocent excitement. "We got the bad guy! That was fun, Musubu!"

And so, our five days living on a deserted island came to an end—not exactly *Two Years' Vacation*, but an adventure nonetheless.

Now I was back to fully enjoying my peaceful summer break.

As expected, Princess Yonaga was incensed. She had hardly been speaking to me at all, aside from grumbling a few things here and there like "Hmph!" and "Just die" and "I hate you."

I smiled through it all, wondering how I ended up with a girl so cute.

According to Haruto, Mr. Kusakabe hadn't disposed of his photobooks after all. He took them back home with him, to the room in his condo that he'd set aside for just that purpose. Placed carefully back on their bookshelves, the books waited to comfort Mr. Kusakabe during the occasional visit.

That day on the island, when Haruto had caught Mr. Kusakabe red-handed, I told the dejected older man something in secret.

"Even if human idols stab you in the back, books will never betray you. Even now, your books love you, and they're worried about you."

If that was enough to change Mr. Kusakabe's feelings toward his photobooks, I was glad to hear it.

Fifteen went back to the town library.

I was passing close by one day, so I popped in, and I heard him from the recommended reading section.

"Earlier, an elementary school boy read me. He stared down at me with big eyes, and when I saw them go wide or shine brightly or tear up or fill with excitement, my heart started pumping, too. It felt like I was going on an adventure! Ah, I wonder what kind of kid will read me next? I hope they all enjoy me lots!"

I stood there with affection in my heart, as if I were Fifteen's older brother.

Yes, yes, you've grown, too, haven't you?

It felt as if I had awakened to the joy that books feel.

"But I still need to have an adventure outside sometimes! Let's go ride a kite together again or get shipwrecked in a stormy sea, Musubu!"

Forgetting that people could see me, I groaned.

"But I'm an indoor person, geez!"

PRINCESS YONAGA'S INNER THOUGHTS

Don't even think about telling Musubu, or else I'll curse ya!

...Musubu left on a trip without me.

o(T∧T o) ｸｩ

...Meanie.

(つд-｡)

...I'll never let him turn my pages again.

(´ ;д;`)

...I hope that jerk Musubu gets swallowed by a whale and never comes back.

(≧□≦;)

...I lied. Get back here already!

°·｡(｡/□＼｡)｡·°

Book
5

The Devotion of "The Surgery Room"

A college student arrived at the small local library, fidgeting nervously. With his glasses and soft, curly hair, plus skin that looked as if it had never seen a tan, he seemed like some sort of young literary enthusiast from the Taisho period at the turn of the twentieth century.

Anxiously checking his surroundings, he headed down the aisle between the bookshelves. He passed by the history section and slinked stealthily past the folklore studies books. This was his usual route. Once a week, at three o'clock in the afternoon on Tuesdays, he stood there in front of one particular shelf.

He headed to the modern Japanese literature section without fail, where the masterpieces of the Meiji and Showa periods lined the shelves. There he eyed one particular book with affection and bashfulness, gently pulled it off the shelf with his pale fingers, and smiled slightly as if meeting an old friend.

On this day, however, when signs of the coming autumn had begun to fill the air, the book he loved was not in its usual place.

His habit was to borrow the book and take it home, return it one week later on the next Tuesday, then borrow the same book again the following week. It was a pattern he had kept to for an entire year. Today was the day he was supposed to borrow the book.

But the book in question was not where it belonged!

All the books in the modern literature section were old and heavy hardcover volumes, so they were hardly ever checked out. There was a copy of the book he was looking for in the paperback section, too, and that one was more popular.

The book was likely still somewhere in the building. But what if it had been lent out? If he was unlucky, he wouldn't be able to see it for two weeks.

Such a hardship would be too much to bear. He stood there staring at the place where his beloved book had been, eyes clouded with despair—

"Um, are you looking for this book by any chance?"

"Eeeek!"

When I spoke to him, the college student shrieked like a little girl in surprise and peered back timidly through his glasses. I held up the book so that he could see the cover. Once he noticed the bulky hardcover in my hands, the young man's eyes widened.

"Ah!"

Nodding his head rapidly, he made another noise and blushed bright red before my eyes.

The book in my hands seemed to have noticed his skittish reaction. She whispered shyly:

"Sir Mejirogawa...I am so pleased to see you."

I'm in high school—my name is Musubu Enoki, and I can hear the voices of books and speak with them.

I'm a regular at all the libraries that dot the area around my school and home, and most of the books there recognize my face. When I pass them by, they make sure to greet me.

"Musubu, haven't seen you in a while!"

"Good afternoon, Musubu."

When no one else is around, I greet them back with a "Hey" or an "It's been a while," and when there are other people, I try to wave a little and smile with my eyes.

One day after the start of the second semester, I casually made a stop at one of my regular libraries after school. When I got there, I heard a number of voices rising from the area where ancient, middle, and modern Japanese literature was shelved.

"We were waiting for you, Musubu!"

"Musubu, would you listen to her problem for us?"

"Consider this a request from the rest of us, too. We want you to lend her a hand, Musubu."

As usual, there were hardly any people in that section, so I lowered my voice and asked, "What happened? I'll help if there's anything I can do."

They told me they wanted me to advise a certain tome in matters of romance.

Furthermore, her partner was a young man, a university student.

University student?

So you're telling me this book fell in love with a human?

"Musubu, we thought you of all people would understand the love between a human and a book, right? I mean, you do have experience."

Sure enough, it was just as they said. I had fallen hard for a book with an indigo cover and became her boyfriend. The young princess had a jealous streak and accused me of cheating if I even touched another book, before grousing about how my conduct was "unacceptable." So on this day, she was staying at home.

"You're going to see...some other book, aren't you...? You heartbreaker..."

When I told her I was going, she sulked and dismissed me with such contempt that it made my chest constrict.

"...If you touch another book, you can die for all I care."

Well, I took that as proof that she loves me, in her own way.

Anyway—that's enough about me.

I decided to first speak with the book that was in love with the college student.

The title embossed into the thick spine read The Surgery Room.

It was written by Kyōka Izumi, a literary master who gifted the world with a number of fantastical stories from the end of the Meiji period into the Showa period. "The Surgery Room" is a short story that tells the tale of a beautiful countess who is concealing an affair between herself and the doctor who is going to be operating on her.

To be more precise, the book who needed my help was an anthology of Kyōka's works. In addition to "The Surgery Room," *she* included a number of other titles, like "The Holy Man of Mount Koya," "The Righteous and the Chivalrous," *Demon Lake*, "Grass Labyrinth," and *Terihakyougen*. All of them were masterpieces.

But when I spoke with *her*, the personality—er, character—of the book seemed strongly influenced by the title story, "The Surgery Room," so I decided to call her Miss Surgery—Surge for short.

"It was exactly one year ago this fall when I first met the student with gentle hands, Michihisa Mejirogawa."

In a graceful, refined voice just like the one belonging to the countess in "The Surgery Room," Surge told me all about this Mejirogawa.

"He stopped and stood before this shelf and gazed at every title, as if searching for something.

"When he got to me, his eyes came to a stop, and he blushed just slightly, like he had found what he was looking for. He stared at me passionately for a while.

"The student touched me gently, as if I were a precious object that mustn't be dirtied. He reached out timidly with both hands, then brought me close to his chest. I could almost feel his profound happiness."

Surge told me that on that day, the student had borrowed her from the library, then taken her home to his single-room apartment where he lived alone. They had spent a lovely night together.

As soon as he got home, he had pulled Surge out of his bag and hugged her tightly to his chest again. Then he opened her cover more gently than anyone ever had before and read her word by word with bleary, delirious eyes, which he sometime let drift closed as he let out a sweet sigh.

After he was finished reading "The Surgery Room," he had embraced the book once more. That night, Surge had slept in his single bed, feeling the warmth of his body.

Somehow, their relationship was sweet from the very beginning.

Surge fell for him completely.

She had been on the library shelf for quite a long time and been read by all sorts, but there had never been anyone who had touched her so gently, sighed so sweetly while reading her, or held her so tenderly.

Their wonderful affair continued night and day for two weeks, right up to the last second of the lending period, so she thought it must be true love.

Even under normal circumstances, books were extremely earnest and genuine creatures.

After that, university student Michihisa Mejirogawa visited the library regularly to borrow Surge. Since he showed up on Tuesdays at three PM like clockwork, he must not have had any work or lectures at that time.

Because it wasn't possible to keep borrowing a single book continuously, he would return her after a week, then check her out again a week later.

Perhaps he was embarrassed to borrow the exact same book every time, because when he took her up to the counter, he would sometimes bring one or two other books with him. Surge told me he never even read the extra books.

What's more, the young man had only leafed through the other stories in the volume once and then never read them again. Instead, he remained entirely focused on reading "The Surgery Room" over and over.

That treatment probably resulted in Surge developing the kind of personality she had now. Her current state was the result of her desire to please the person she loved. Books are very admirable things in that way.

The other books probably couldn't help but be moved by Surge's innocent affection. That's why they had sought out my cooperation.

"As far as I can tell, Mejirogawa and Surge seem to be in love with each other. If not, I doubt he would have kept borrowing the same book for a year."

If he just wanted to read "The Surgery Room," he could have bought a copy in a bookstore or online. Assuming he was working a part-time job as a university student, he should have been able to afford a single book.

The fact that he instead borrowed Surge and only Surge suggested that there was some reason why a different copy would not do.

Mejirogawa was always taking Surge home to his apartment to embrace her, sigh sweetly over her, and sleep with her in his bed, so it was fair to assume he liked her a lot. It was certainly possible he was even in love.

I knew that because I was also in love with a book, one named Princess Yonaga.

There was one important difference, though: I could hear Princess Yonaga's voice, while Mejirogawa probably couldn't hear Surge. But he was nevertheless unmistakably obsessed with her.

"But Sir Mejirogawa has been acting strange lately. His sighs that used to be sweet now sound sorrowful, and he looks away from me while biting his lip as if distressed. Then he grabs his head and rolls around on the floor wailing about something."

The last time she had stayed with him, he had embraced her and sobbed, spilling big, heavy tears.

He hadn't been eating much, barely slept at night, and was so haggard that she found it painful to look at him.

"In this book's body, I can't do anything but watch, even if he is suffering. It's intolerable. I can't stand it. I was wondering if you might speak with Sir Mejirogawa, Sir Musubu, and dispel his troubles."

The other books repeated her request.

"Please, Musubu, I'm asking you, too."

"Me too. If things stay like this, she'll go to pieces worrying over him."

It sounded like if I could resolve Mejirogawa's problem, then Surge could go back to sweetly whiling away the hours with him every other week.

"Sure, I understand. I am a voice for books, after all. I'll start by talking to Mejirogawa. Tomorrow happens to be Tuesday, too."

* * *

—Taking up the task with my usual enthusiasm, I feigned sick the next day in my sixth period class so I could leave early and get to the library by three. There I waited on standby with Surge in hand.

Taken aback when an unfamiliar high school student with glasses came out of nowhere to strike up a conversation, Mejirogawa asked, "H-how did you know I was looking for that book?"

"Because I've seen you borrowing it all the time. I'm a regular at this library, you see. Whenever we're both here, I think, 'Oh, there he goes borrowing "The Surgery Room" again.'"

At these words, Mejirogawa flushed deep red. "I-is it that obvious?"

"No, that's not what I meant. See, I also like this book a lot. I'm a big fan of Kyōka Izumi, and 'The Surgery Room' is my favorite. So I thought maybe I'd try speaking with you, since you're a Kyōka fan, too."

Good, that doesn't sound too unnatural, as far as excuses go. Plus, it's true that I'm a regular here and that I'm a Kyōka fan. My favorite is actually "Grass Labyrinth," though.

"Oh, is that it?"

His expression brightened a little but then suddenly shifted again.

"!" He opened his eyes wide, as if he had spotted something behind me, then turned beet red and started fidgeting nervously.

Huh? Wait? What's going on?

He looks like he's in love— What? With me*?! Is he reading too much into this because we both wear glasses and like Kyōka Izumi or something? Aaahhh!*

As I started to panic, a clear voice called out from behind me.

"Enoki, you're here quite early today, aren't you?"

A lovely and modest-looking young woman wearing an apron smiled gently.

Her name was Fumina Suzue, and she was one of the librarians here.

"Good afternoon. There was a book I wanted to borrow, so I rushed over."

"Oh, that book?" Ms. Suzue looked down at my hands. Her eyes went wide.

"Yes, I'll—I'll take this one."

I turned to look for Mejirogawa, but he had already backed off about two meters and was still creeping away. Maybe he was embarrassed to be seen blushing so brightly, because he slunk off with his head hung low, his shoulders hunched, and his eyes on the ground.

Hang on, wait—

What's this? What's going on?

He disappeared behind a faraway bookcase before I had a chance to call out and stop him. I caught a glimpse of his profile, and he was red all the way out to his ears.

"Enoki, was the young man just now an acquaintance of yours?" the librarian asked.

"Huh? Um, I just met him a minute ago, but—"

"I see. He always borrows *The Surgery Room*, so I think he probably wanted it," she answered in an amused tone, looking down at the book in my hands.

Though Mejirogawa had been borrowing other books to disguise his checkout history, it sounded as though the librarians had nevertheless pegged him as the "the 'Surgery Room' guy."

More importantly, that blushing young maiden act he put on was something else...

"Whenever Lady Suzue is at the counter, Sir Mejirogawa gets extremely bashful."

Surge cheerlessly informed me of this in my arms.

Huh? So that means he always reacts like that in front of her?

His face goes bright red, he chokes up, and he can't make eye contact the whole time he's checking out?

Waaait a sec, that definitely sounds like he's in love with Ms. Suzue!

But he's doing his best to keep it together in front of Surge.

She must have realized it, too...

Hmm, this just got a lot more complicated.

Furthermore, I could see something sparkling brightly on the edge of my vision. On the ring finger of Ms. Suzue's slender hand was what appeared to be a glittering diamond band.

She was unmarried, as far as I could recall. I had never seen her wearing it before.

"That ring! Ms. Suzue, are you getting married?" I asked.

She broke into a bashful smile. "Yes. The ceremony isn't until next year, but we decided to go ahead and add me to his family register. We're moving into our new home next month, so we'll take care of the formalities then."

"Congratulations! You're so pretty, I bet a lot of the library regulars are really going to be upset, huh?" I asked jokingly. "Actually, I'm kind of upset myself."

She laughed it off quickly. "Oh my, thank you! But you're the only one who's said anything."

Hmm—either Ms. Suzue isn't aware of Mejirogawa's feelings for her or she's realized how he feels but is choosing to ignore it.

Nevertheless, I had ascertained that Mejirogawa was crying alone in his apartment because the librarian he was in love with was getting married.

In my hands, Surge, who had requested that I clear up whatever was troubling Mejirogawa, murmured weepily, **"Sir Mejirogawa...you poor thing..."**

A love triangle?

No, a love...square?

What can I do to help here?

The following day after school, I visited a café one station before the library where Ms. Suzue worked. The place sold pancakes and waffles prettily plated and Instagram-worthy latte art, so it seemed to be popular with girls.

"Welcome. Ah! You're—!"

Wearing a shirt and pants that could be mistaken for street clothes, but with a black apron tied around his waist marking him as a waiter, was a man with curly, fluffy hair and glasses— Mejirogawa widened his eyes.

I played dumb. "Oh? You work here?"

"Yeah. Enoki...right? What a coincidence."

A coincidence, right.

I smiled as I took my seat and put in an order for the "Angel's Breath Fluffy Pancake Set."

Of course, this was no coincidence. Surge had told me that Mejirogawa was working part-time at this café.

The day before, I had borrowed Surge and taken her home with me.

I had wanted to have another proper conversation with her, in a setting where we could speak freely.

Princess Yonaga was waiting in my bedroom, so normally I would have headed straight for my older sister's room—she was in medical school in Hokkaido. But that day, I decided to talk in my room instead.

"I'm home, Princess Yonaga."

The moment I greeted her, she responded so frigidly that it sent shivers down my spine.

"...I smell another woman."

Ah, perceptive as always. And she's about to switch into "darkness mode."

The indigo paperback that I had left on top of a lace handkerchief spread out on the bed seemed to almost radiate cold air.

"Yep, today I invited Miss Surge here to come home with me."

I pulled the heavy hardcover book from my bag, got down on my knee beside the bed, and held her cover to cover with Princess Yonaga.

"Lovely to meet you. I am an anthology of the works of Kyōka Izumi, and normally I reside at the local library. Today I have an urgent need to consult with Sir Musubu regarding the man I love, so I've taken the liberty of intruding on your home."

"......"

"I have heard that you are Sir Musubu's beloved sweetheart, Princess. Some of the other books and I aspire to be like you. Despite being a book, you've fallen in love with your reader Sir Musubu, and the two of you live a happy life like this together."

"......"

"Princess Yonaga, you are an inspiration to all texts who have fallen for our readers. I am simply delighted to have met you."

"......"

Princess Yonaga had stayed silent the whole time. Of course, normally she would be launching into a tirade about "infidelity" and "adulterers" and "dancing on graves," so she must have deemed the presence of Surge acceptable because she only had eyes for another man.

Surge's dilemma probably bored her. On the other hand, she likely did have some interest in the outcome of a romance between a book and a human. When I started talking to Surge, I could tell that the princess was straining to listen.

"Surge, you knew Mejirogawa likes Ms. Suzue."

"Yes... Whenever Sir Mejirogawa comes to the library, he always searches for her. His eyes fill with happiness as he stares at her from gaps between the books on the shelves or around the ends of the stacks. It's the same look he gets reading me at home," Surge answered with reservation. I pictured a beautiful young woman with pale skin, elegant yet modest, speaking with downturned eyes.

"Suppose things had gone well between Mejirogawa and Ms. Suzue, and they had become lovers; what were you planning to do?"

"I don't know. I'm a book, so...all I can do is watch over the person I care about. But if that's the case, I would rather see Sir Mejirogawa smiling happily than suffering."

She was too noble for her own good.

It was heart-wrenching.

As expected, Princess Yonaga had been silent as she listened to Surge's beautiful musings.

"......"

I'd gotten the feeling the princess was internally deriding the other woman for being a naive, helpless fool. I was glad she didn't mock her out loud.

So that was how Surge had reasserted her request to me and why I had come to Mejirogawa's place of employment.

When he brought over my order of fluffy pancakes and a caffe latte with an angel drawn in the foam, I questioned him without pretense.

"By the way, you like Ms. Suzue from the library, right?"

He nearly dumped my latte all over the table.

"H-h-h-h-h-how did you—?"

"It's pretty obvious."

"Huh?! That means Ms. Suzue must have noticed, too— Aaah, what do I do?" Hugging the tray, he seemed close to collapsing on the floor in distress.

I reassured him. "I think you'll be fine as long as you stop slinking around and act normal around her. I don't think it bothers her."

"You're right...," he mumbled despondently. "A girl like her would never bother with a guy like me at all..." I could practically see his ears drooping like a dog. "I don't even think she remembers that I exist..."

Doesn't remember you?

Didn't I see you two having a conversation?

"Um, if you need me to lend an ear , I'll listen."

One hour later—

Once he was finished working, Mejirogawa removed his apron and pulled up a seat at my café table. Sorrowfully, he told me about how he met Ms. Suzue and developed a heartbreaking, one-sided love for her.

Actually, should we take this somewhere else? The cook at the counter and all his coworkers are looking over here with pity.

They can definitely hear us, and they're definitely listening.

But Mejirogawa kept talking, as if his goddess—Ms. Suzue—were the only person who existed in his world.

"That book was what made me fall in love with her. At the time, I was only ten years old, in fourth grade. They were holding public readings at the library, and that one happened to catch my interest, so I went. But it wasn't geared toward children, and everyone there was much older than me, all high schoolers and college kids and adults."

Since he was the only elementary schooler in a small group, he had stuck out like a sore thumb and had curled up bashfully in his chair out of embarrassment.

But when Ms. Suzue, who was a college student at the time, had held the heavy hardcover book in her delicate hands, turned the page, and started reading—

* * *

"The surgery was to take place at a certain hospital in the Tokyo suburbs, and the Countess Kifune was the patient on whom my dear friend Doctor Takamine was to perform the operation. Driven by curiosity, I imposed upon Takamine to allow me to attend. In order to present my case as strongly as possible, I concocted an argument about my being an artist and why seeing the surgery would be useful to me."

She read out the beautiful passage in her graceful, soothing voice.

Mejirogawa told me that it sounded just like water flowing smoothly down a river with no breaks, clear and sparkling, absorbing and reflecting rays of light from the sun.

Characteristic of Kyōka Izumi's style of writing, there were many passages where the meaning of the words wasn't immediately apparent on first reading. Add to that the fact that he was a fourth grader, and Mejirogawa hadn't gotten much of the story at all.

Even so, the words that flowed one by one like a sequence of glittering glass marbles from the mouth of the pretty older girl with pale skin and a kind face had been bewitchingly beautiful, and he'd found himself drawn in, utterly entranced.

"And there in the center of the room lay the Countess Kifune, focus of concern for both those outside the room and those inside, who were closely observing her. Wrapped in a spotless white hospital gown, she lay on the operating table as if a corpse—face drained of color, nose pointing upward, chin narrow and frail, and her arms and legs seeming too fragile to bear even the weight of fine silk. Her teeth were slightly visible between pale lips. Her eyes were tightly closed, and her eyebrows drawn with worry. Loosely bound, her hair fell lightly across her pillow and spilled down on the operating table."

Pure sensuality—

It must have been the first time the young fourth grader had felt such things stirring inside him. The college girl reading "The Surgery Room" aloud had looked as pure and holy as the Virgin Mary, and her voice had been soft and graceful. But something had been equally frightening about the beautiful words that spilled out every time she opened her light-pink lips, and it sent a shiver up his spine.

He had wanted to listen to her forever, feeling that shiver all the while.

That was what he had thought, he told me.

When the public reading was over, he had been too dazed to stand up from his chair. The college girl had approached the young Mejirogawa, holding the book she had just read to her chest.

Once she'd reached him, she bent her knees a little so that she could look him in the face and spoke to him with gentle eyes.

"I guess that was difficult for an elementary schooler, huh? Try reading it again when you're a little older, okay? It's a harsh but wonderful tale. My favorite short story, in fact."

His heart had been threatening to explode out of his chest, so he had only managed to get a few words in.

"Okay, I'll read it. I'll definitely read it."

The older girl had smiled chastely.

"I'm happy to hear that."

"And that was Ms. Suzue?"

"Yeah, after that, I tried reading 'The Surgery Room' right away, but the sentences are long and there are a lot of difficult kanji, so it was totally incomprehensible to me. And then we moved because my dad got transferred at work, and I couldn't go to that library anymore, so I didn't have any other chance to get my hands on the book..."

Now that he was in university, Mejirogawa had, entirely by chance, started living alone on the same train route as the library from his memories, and he had stopped in for old times' sake exactly a year ago—last autumn.

He told me that he had sought out the same hardcover volume Ms. Suzue had read from and that he was elated when he found it.

He'd signed up for a library card, checked out the book, and taken it home with him. Reading it had filled his mind with Ms. Suzue's voice and likeness and sent his heart into overdrive.

Then two weeks later, when Mejirogawa had gone to the library to return the book, he saw Ms. Suzue, who was working there as a librarian, again. He'd started trembling the moment he caught sight of her working behind the counter and had apparently gone out of his way to line up in front of a different librarian. Though he tried countless times after that, he hadn't been able to so much as look her in the eye.

"Why didn't you let her know you were the elementary schooler she spoke kindly to at the public reading? What would have been wrong about that?"

Surely Ms. Suzue would be happy to know that Mejirogawa had borrowed and read "The Surgery Room" as a college student.

"I've tried so many times. But whenever I glimpse her face, I blank out, and I turn white as a sheet. Even when *she makes the first move* at the counter by thanking me for returning my books, I get so nervous, I start shaking."

Well, I wouldn't call that making a move, more like she's just doing her job.

"I'm much younger than her…and I know it would cause problems…to be with a library patron…"

His cheeks reddened, and he looked down at the ground, squirming.

This guy is a real shrinking violet.

"B-besides, she's getting married! Aaaaahhh!"

"Ah! Please don't cry!"

I handed him a napkin, and he blotted his eyes.

"S-sorry," he apologized. But his eyes were already flooding with salty tears.

Oh no. All your coworkers are looking at you. They seem worried!

Even if he hadn't been able to bring himself to approach Ms. Suzue, his secret was obvious to anyone paying attention.

It was safe to assume Ms. Suzue had noticed it, too.

The fact that she has been treating him the same as all the other patrons must mean she isn't interested… Hmm, no surprise there. She's gorgeous, so she must have always been pretty popular. I'm sure she knows a thing or two about dealing with unrequited love.

She mentioned moving into her new home and getting entered into her husband's family register next month.

There's almost no chance Ms. Suzue would ever get involved with Mejirogawa once she's married.

Actually, even now, it's practically zero.

Hmmm……

After mulling it over for a short while, I turned to Mejirogawa, whose eyes were like a bleary Chihuahua's, and asked him point-blank, "How about confessing your love to Ms. Suzue?"

"Whaaaaaat?!"

He was taken aback.

Most of the other wait staff at the café were leaning in to watch the show.

"I told you, she's getting married—she's someone's wife! She's got a ring and everything!"

"That's exactly why! Before she gets entered into the family register and her name changes, you've got to tell her that you met her when you were a kid and that you've loved her ever since. If you do that, you'll feel a weight off your shoulders, and even though she'll turn you down, you'll be able to move forward, right?"

His coworkers had all gathered around our table. They nodded in his stead.

"Mejirogawa," I continued, "when I look at you, I worry that if Ms. Suzue gets married without you having confessed, the secret will weigh you down forever, and you'll spend night after night crying into your pillow."

His coworkers nodded again, enthusiastic.

"I know we just met—sorry for being so forward," I added.

Surge had requested that I help Mejirogawa regain his smile.

"I'm a book, so...all I can do is watch over the person I care about. But if that's the case, I would rather see Sir Mejirogawa smiling happily than suffering."

* * *

Ms. Suzue rejecting Mejirogawa would definitely hurt, but I reckoned he would feel surprisingly at ease after the fact.

"But I'll just cause trouble for Ms. Suzue."

"Sure you would, if you pressured her to break up with her fiancé and marry you instead or something."

"Wha—?! I w-w-w-w-would never say something so aggressive!"

"Of course you wouldn't. So there's no problem."

I grinned.

"First, you tell her that her public reading of 'The Surgery Room' deeply touched you when you were an elementary school student. Then you continue on to say you fell in love with her back then, so you got butterflies when you were reintroduced and realized she was your childhood crush. Try to keep it light when you talk to her. It won't do any good to burden her with the knowledge that you cried when you learned she was getting married or that she was your first love. You want to wish her happiness—the key point is to keep your conversation cheerful to the end. If you can manage that, she'll be able to laugh your confession off with a smile and maybe even feel flattered that it was a cute college boy who told her."

"Yeah…yeah, maybe…"

All right! He's coming around to confessing.

"Definitely. I'll help, too, and we'll create an atmosphere where it's easy to talk to her. Let's do it—a love confession ten years in the making!"

Mejirogawa's coworkers all crowded around, shouting in encouragement.

"That's the spirit! You can do it, Micchi!"

"I think I should confess, too!"

"Show her what you got, Micchi!"

So Mejirogawa is called Micchi, huh…? I guess his name is Michihisa…

"Micchi" finally nodded. "O-okay. I'll confess to her."

Two days later, on Friday—

I bolted to the library after school, where I struck up a conversation with Ms. Suzue as she walked down the aisles pushing a cart laden with books.

"Ms. Suzue, did you know that a new book in the Golden Rule series by Hisa Hayakawa is coming out?"

"What? Really? I love that series. I've got all of them at home!"

"I heard it's going on sale next spring."

"That's quite a ways off."

"I suppose you'll already be a married woman by then. Oh! Mejirogawa!"

I made a big show of waving to Mejirogawa, who was standing way behind Ms. Suzue, fidgeting nervously.

He awkwardly shuffled toward us.

"Look, his right arm and right leg are moving in sync."
"He's dripping with sweat."
"You got this, young man!"

Waves of encouragement erupted from the books packed onto the cart.

Inside, I was also rooting for him.

That's right—get in there! Act a little more natural. If you get lost, just smile and start talking.

"H-hey, Enoki. You came."

"Yeah, it's rare to see you here at the library on a Friday."

"I...suppose...it is."

Mejirogawa couldn't bring himself to look in her direction at all. Instead, his eyes kept darting around unnaturally.

Ah, this might not work.

We had decided ahead of time that I would strike up a conversation with Ms. Suzue first, then Mejirogawa would join us. We had even outlined our chat, but the script had probably completely flown out of his head.

I've got to guide him. I don't see any other way out.

"Mejirogawa, don't you always come here on Tuesdays? And I always see you checking out the Kyōka Izumi anthology with 'The Surgery Room,' right? Is there some reason for that?"

"It's, it's because—"

His face was visibly reddening.

Ms. Suzue anxiously awaited his answer.

"That's because, um…uh…the thing is, you see—"

"Uh-oh, he's losing it!"

"Get it together, man!"

I was nearly squirming, too.

If he delivered an anguished declaration of love as if it was a matter of life and death, Ms. Suzue would be frightened at best and disturbed at worst.

Just as I was debating whether to call the whole thing off, Mejirogawa spat out a few words, still looking down at the floor.

"…I was thinking about writing about 'The Surgery Room' for my university thesis…so, well, I'll be taking this."

He bowed sharply and quickly scurried away.

Ms. Suzue looked puzzled but understanding. "I see. So that's why he is always borrowing the book, huh?"

"I'm sorry! I'm sorry!"

When I found Mejirogawa hanging his head in a corner of the library, he started bowing and apologizing before I could even get a word in.

"…Mejirogawa, I'm repeating myself now, but you can't talk to Ms. Suzue like you're obsessed with her. You've got to keep it light and natural to the end. The idea is that you're telling her about fleeting feelings of first love from your boyhood days. If you make her think you're a stalker or make her feel threatened, that's going to end badly for you, too, right?"

"Guh!"

"Talk to her normally."

Mejirogawa moved to bow and apologize but suddenly held his tongue and stared up at me, still doubled over at the waist.

"Like the way I talk to Mrs. Shimazaki?"

"Mrs. Shimazaki…as in Ms. Suzue's coworker? The one who celebrated her fiftieth birthday recently? Whose three-year-old granddaughter drew her a picture for a present? That Mrs. Shimazaki?"

He nodded.

"Mrs. Shimazaki has a son who's a college student and the same age as me, so she remembers my name. When it's raining, she'll lend me one of the library umbrellas and say it's okay to take it home. Once when I had a cold and a bad cough, she gave me some medicine and told me to drink it and keep warm while resting up at home. She's nurturing and kind, so even I can talk to her without getting nervous."

She really likes Mejirogawa, huh…?

Though I doubt he feels the same way about a plump, middle-aged woman of fifty as he does about Ms. Suzue, who's still young and slim.

"Oh, that's it! You've got to think of Ms. Suzue as Mrs. Shimazaki and try again. Got it? Ms. Suzue is Mrs. Shimazaki, Mrs. Shimazaki, Mrs. Shimazaki…"

"Mrs. Shimazaki, Mrs. Shimazaki, Mrs. Shimazaki…" He repeated her name like a spell.

"Ready? Here we go."

Just as he started to walk over after I confirmed that Ms. Suzue was still there pushing her cart, Mejirogawa suddenly crouched down behind me. His face was bright red, and his breathing was ragged, as if he had just finished a marathon.

"Hah…haaah…I j-just can't do it. Ms. Suzue is nothing like Mrs. Shimazaki," he muttered, tearing up.

What a total shrinking violet!

"I'm sorry, Enoki, my heart just isn't ready… I'll do better next time. I'm really sorry. I can't skip any more work than I already have, so I've got to go. I'm sorry, I'm sorry!"

Mejirogawa hurried out of the library, apologizing weakly as he fled.

Yeesh, seems like we have a long road ahead.

Just then—

"Tch, two-timin' jerk."

* * *

A distinctly unfriendly voice from one of the shelves.

That sounds like it's coming from where they keep foreign contemporary literature...

"Yer a good match for those giggling girlies in miniskirts. Say hi to 'em for me! Don't show yer face around here again."

After straining my ears carefully, I pinpointed the source and pulled out the book—a hard-boiled detective novel with pictures of cryptids and roses on the cover. "Are you the one who was talking just now?" I asked.

"Yeah, what of it?"

"Who were you calling a two-timing jerk?"

"That curly-haired guy who was just here. He acts all weak, but he's two-timing for sure."

Mejirogawa is two-timing?

What?! What does that mean?

Still holding the book, I moved into a corner and brought my face close to the cover, then whispered, "Would you give me a little more detail? Who is Mejirogawa two-timing with?"

The book answered in a somewhat sullen, dry voice, **"There's a girl in a miniskirt, a year behind him in university. He had his arms around her earlier, flirting. A young lady who graduated from Yurizono Academy. Heard they're dating."**

"Wait, Mejirogawa said that? He said he was dating her?" I unintentionally raised my voice.

"Enoki? What's wrong?"

Ah, Ms. Suzue!

"N-nothing, it's nothing. I just remembered some urgent business and shouted at myself."

"Use your inside voice in the library, please."

"Sorry."

Ms. Suzue didn't leave right away. She seemed to have something else to say.

It's probably about Mejirogawa. He was acting pretty strange today, and it probably put her on her guard. That could be a problem.

She frowned a little, concerned. "Um...Enoki?"

After starting off hesitantly, as if she couldn't get the words out—

"Never mind, it's fine."

—she smiled politely and went back to the counter.

So it was about Mejirogawa, huh...?

I tried quietly asking the book about its suspicions regarding Mejirogawa's alleged two-timing, but perhaps because Ms. Suzue had told us to lower our voices, the book didn't say another word.

"Huh? A girlfriend in a miniskirt? Me? Huh? Huuuh? When did I get a girlfriend?"

Mejirogawa blinked rapidly in surprise after he brought me my caffe latte. A picture of two little birds kissing had been drawn in the foam.

"I overheard she was a year behind you in school, a fancy girl who graduated from Yurizono Academy. At the...uh, library."

"A year behind me...? Oh! Maybe Ayuhara? Did you hear that from Mrs. Shimazaki?"

I couldn't tell him a book had told me, so I dodged the question.

Apparently, the novel was mistaken about her being his girlfriend. But that must mean an underclassman who attended Yurizono Academy, a fancy girl in a miniskirt, went to the library at some point...

"Once when we were out together on an errand for our club, I stopped in at the library to return a book. When we got there and I was about to turn in the anthology with 'The Surgery Room,' Ayuhara said she wanted to try reading it and borrowed it on the spot."

"Micchi, this is the type of stuff you read? Tell me, is it interesting?"

"Yeah, I really like it. I've borrowed it loads of times."

"Hmm, well then, I think I'll borrow it next!"

* * *

They'd had that exchange at the counter, and the underclassman in the miniskirt, Ayuhara, had taken Surge home with her.

But two weeks later, when Mejirogawa asked how she'd liked it, Ayuhara had answered dismissively:

"It had a lot of kanji, and I didn't really understand it."

He felt as if she'd been avoiding him ever since.

"I guess that book really didn't agree with her… It's too bad."

Mejirogawa seemed pained by the fact that he hadn't gotten her to take a liking to his beloved book. Actually, he looked downright despondent.

"Mrs. Shimazaki asked me once if the girl with me that day was my girlfriend, but I told her no and explained the situation. Maybe she wasn't listening."

The novel that told me about Mejirogawa's alleged two-timing must have seen him with Ayuhara when they came to the library together and assumed she was his girlfriend.

He probably framed it like that because he knew about Surge's devotion to Mejirogawa and got angry seeing him flirt with another girl right in front of her.

To double-check, I said, "So what it comes down to is that the 'two-timing' was all a misunderstanding on Mrs. Shimazaki's part? No question about it?"

"Of course! This is actually the first I've heard about Ayuhara graduating from Yurizono. I've been so focused on Ms. Suzue…"

His face reddened at the mere mention of her name.

This guy is hopeless…

"In that case, stick to the script next time. If you act this suspicious again, you're going to put her totally on guard, okay?"

Never mind the fact that she's probably already got her guard up…

He responded earnestly, "Got it. Ever since the other day, I've been thinking over what you told me before, Enoki. I'd never considered telling Ms. Suzue how I felt about her, but like you said, confessing my love should let me move on with my life. If she's going to be happily married, I want to wish her well from the bottom of my heart."

Ah, Surge said the same thing. That's right… She said she wanted the person she loves to smile.

Holding that feeling close to your heart is a sure sign of a strong, kind person. Mejirogawa may act like a blushing maiden, he might seem hapless and weak, but at his core, he's probably a really solid guy.

"I'm not expecting her to return my affection or anything crazy. I just… I at least want her to remember the day we first met and let her know how much she touched me back then. Being able do that would be plenty."

"I think your wish will come true as soon as you make the effort."

"Right. Okay, I'll do my best." His lips softened into a smile.

It was a friendly smile: gentle and with a real winsomeness to it. Surge was the one who had asked me to counsel him in matters of romance, but at this point, I was genuinely rooting for him myself.

If only I could steer this thing to a conclusion Mejirogawa could accept…

But my hands will be tied if he starts acting fishy in front of Ms. Suzue again.

Ah, that's it!

"Would you consider holding a public reading, Mejirogawa?"

"You're telling me a book asked you to help settle a love affair between humans? That sounds like something you'd get yourself into, Musubu. All right, I'll arrange one of the rooms in the music hall for your use."

On the grounds of Seijou Academy, the school I attended, stood a splendid music hall owned by the orchestra club. I'd asked my friend Haruto, the son of the school chair and director of the orchestra, to borrow a room in the hall for a public reading the following Saturday.

"Thanks so much! Would you like to join us, too?"

"Certainly, I'd definitely like to if I can. I was also thinking it might be nice to invite Tsumashina."

"Tsumashina?"

We were in the same grade but different classes, and I had made her acquaintance through a fateful encounter with a certain book, just like

I had met Haruto. She looked intimidating and spoke rudely, which reminded me a little of my older sister, who was away at medical school in Hokkaido.

But why her?

Haruto put on a sly smile. "She asked me if the reason you're always dashing off after school is because you're seeing someone..."

Ah, so the rumors about having girlfriends have gotten around to me, too?

The truth is that I'm already taken—by a book I call Princess Yonaga. But recently, I had been spending all my time with Mejirogawa and hadn't had the time to hang out with Haruto.

Besides, I had Surge at my house now, too.

"I went ahead and told her that I didn't think you were the type to have a casual fling. I suggested that if she wants to set the record straight on your girlfriend, she'd better ask you herself. Though she brushed it off and said she didn't really care."

"I'm sure she was just making small talk."

"I wonder..."

Haruto smiled coyly again, but if he'd seen how Tsumashina acted toward me on a daily basis, it would have blown any suspicions of his right out of the water.

"Well, thanks for arranging the meeting room."

"Of course. Although this time, I think I'll ask for something a little different as payment."

Ah, I knew that was coming.

That same day, I went to the library and found Ms. Suzue reshelving returned books from her cart.

I told her we were planning on holding a public reading at my school and that I wanted her to attend as well. She seemed reluctant, but I persisted. "The theme of the reading is Kyōka Izumi's 'The Surgery Room.' I invited Mejirogawa, too, so please come. Actually, I think he wanted to invite you himself the other day, but he's too shy. He said he gets nervous in front of beautiful women like you."

That's all it took to get what I wanted. She was probably intrigued by the chance to take a look at our school library, which apparently housed many valuable books.

"I understand. I finish work here at three o'clock that day, so I can come after that."

"Thank you so much. We'll see you at four."

I told her I would message her the details, and we exchanged contact information on LINE. As I watched Ms. Suzue push her cart away, I heaved a sigh of relief.

"So you're into older women, huh, Enoki?"

To my surprise, Tsumashina had been watching me, schoolbag hanging off one shoulder and a sour look on her face.

"Wah! What are you doing here?" I yelped. My glasses slipped down my nose again, and I pushed them back into place.

"I just thought I might do my homework in the library," Tsumashina answered bluntly, with a hint of unease.

If you're going to do that, the school library is both quieter and more spacious. You'd probably get more work done there.

At first, I simply acknowledged her statement, but then I decided to correct her earlier assumption. "Besides, I prefer younger women over older, I think."

"Ew, what, like a pedo?"

"No, like my girlfriend is younger than me, is all."

Technically, she was quite a bit older if you went off the publishing date, but in my mind, Princess Yonaga was a younger girl skilled at getting people to spoil her.

And that's how she *was, Princess Yonaga's former owner, so—*

Tsumashina's jaw dropped when she heard that I had a girlfriend. Then she scrunched her lips down tightly and drew the corners of her mouth up in a slight smile.

"What a surprise. You, a girlfriend? And I guess you relax and have your dates at home on the weekends?"

"She's sulky 'cause I've been busy lately, which is rough."

"Are you humblebragging?" She pouted again. "So this younger girlfriend of yours, what type is she anyway?"

"Hmm... I'd have to say she's a princess, I guess."

"What? A princess?" Tsumashina's eyes shot wide-open. "Oh, no way! Some young, sweet, pure princess in a poofy white dress? Talk about cliché! You want the same thing as every other guy!" She was really getting pissed. "Well, your love life's got nothing to do with me, Enoki, so I couldn't care less. I mean, I just got a love confession from a second-year boy who asked me to be his girlfriend."

"Oh yeah?"

There was nothing wrong with that, but it did surprise me. I mean, I knew Tsumashina was both popular and beautiful, but her personality could be awfully grating.

After the sexual harassment incident in the first semester with Mr. Takekawa, people had been all too happy to gossip about her being too ferocious to be anyone's girlfriend. Since this had really hurt her, I thought it was great that she'd found someone who appreciated her.

Tsumashina seemed to cheer up a little at my surprise. "He's tall and good-looking and a regular member of a sports club, and he's super popular with the girls," she boasted.

"Wow..."

I wasn't sure how to answer, so I made a dull noise of acknowledgment, and her face lit up again. She must have been quite happy to have gotten a love confession from an upperclassman.

I bet she bothered to ask Haruto about me because she wanted to find me and brag about it.

Well, if she likes this upperclassman back, then I'm happy for her. And I'm sure Pip is happy, too, looking down on her owner from above.

"By the way, Tsumashina, are you free next Saturday at four o'clock? I'm borrowing a room in the music hall for a public reading. Do you want to go?"

"Is your girlfriend coming, too?"

"No, I don't think she'll be able to make it."

"I see. I'll think about it. Give me your contact info."

Once I had exchanged LINE information with Tsumashina and we had parted ways, Mrs. Shimazaki, the librarian, asked with a smirk, "My, my, is that girl your girlfriend, Enoki? Making plans for a date? How nice."

This was the woman whom Mejirogawa had said he always felt he could talk to and who had recently had her fiftieth birthday. Mrs. Shimazaki liked looking after other people and loved to chat, so she often talked to me as well.

"No, she's not my girlfriend, and there's no date."

"It's all right; you don't have to be embarrassed."

She's totally convinced that Tsumashina is my girlfriend. Ah, I bet this is how Mejirogawa's schoolmate in the miniskirt became his "girlfriend," too.

"It's the truth. I'm holding a public reading next Saturday, so I was inviting her to that. Ms. Suzue said she would come, too, so if you've got the time—"

"Oh, sorry, I've got work that day. Sure sounds fun, though. What story are you reading?"

"'The Surgery Room.'"

At those words, Mrs. Shimazaki's eyes went wide, and she said something I didn't expect: "My goodness, I'm surprised Suzue accepted, seeing as how she hates that book."

I didn't get home until after dark.

I trudged up the stairs to my room on the second floor with a pit in my stomach, worrying over how to handle the public reading.

I'm at a loss... What on earth is the right thing to do...?

No matter how I thought about it, I couldn't see any conclusion that would make everyone happy.

Far from it, everyone was probably going to end up suffering.

I stood in front of my door, let out a sigh that couldn't be heard from inside, then stepped into my room.

"I'm home, Princess Yonaga, Surge."

"Welcome home, Sir Musubu."

"......"

Surge greeted me gracefully. Princess Yonaga was silent again today, but it seemed the two ladies—the two books, that is—had exchanged words while I was away.

"This afternoon, I had a lovely conversation with Princess Yonaga."

Surge's statement took me by surprise.

Before Princess Yonaga had come to live at my house, all my books that had been in my room had complained to me about her. They were so afraid of the princess that they didn't even want to be in the same room as her.

"Princess Yonaga has shown great concern and kindness to me. Besides, she's so devoted and adorable. It's only natural that you love her, Sir Musubu."

I couldn't believe my ears.

When I asked her just what on earth they had talked about, Princess Yonaga suddenly started clearing her throat loudly. Surge smiled.

"It's a secret."

She wasn't going to tell me.

"Sir Musubu, how is Sir Mejirogawa doing? Was he able let Lady Suzue know how he feels?"

"Well, about that...," I answered hesitantly. "We decided to hold a public reading next Saturday."

I told her we would have the participants take turns reading from "The Surgery Room," and both Mejirogawa and Ms. Suzue had accepted the invitation.

"Well, that sounds like a splendid plan. If she reads aloud from me, Lady Suzue will probably remember Sir Mejirogawa."

Surge was cheerful.

"Besides that, the setting will surely make it easier for Sir Mejirogawa to tell Lady Suzue that he met her when he was in elementary school."

She was thinking only of Mejirogawa, not herself.

I winced at her incredibly admirable attitude.

But if I were to tell Surge what I heard from Mrs. Shimazaki today...it would probably depress her...

"Say, Surge?"

"Yes, what is it?"

"Remember when I asked you something earlier? About what you were planning to do if Mejirogawa and Ms. Suzue were to start a relationship?"

"Yes..."

"And you answered that you didn't know but that you would rather see Mejirogawa happy than see him suffering, so you wanted me to help him, right? If—just if—Mejirogawa were to forget about you, Surge, and never pick you up again, what would you do?"

"Ah..." Surge gasped slightly.

Princess Yonaga was listening carefully. "......"

It was a cruel question. I really felt as if I was going to cry.

"For instance, I think it's possible that once Ms. Suzue rejects him, Mejirogawa might not want to go to the library anymore and might not ever want to read 'The Surgery Room' again. Or consider the opposite situation. If the two of them were to get together, he might no longer need the story in place of her and could forget about you."

After a short silence, Surge answered me gently.

"If that happens—I'll remember him."

It was an earnest voice.

A sincere voice.

"I won't forget him. Not ever."

* * *

Even if the person she loved forgot all about her, she would remember him. That's why this was okay.

That thought made my chest tighten again.

My throat caught.

I really thought I was about to start crying, but I desperately resisted—

I resolved to prepare myself as well.

No matter what the reading on Saturday brough to light, no matter the final result, I would be a voice for Surge.

It was the day of the public reading. Five of us had gathered in the room Haruto had prepared—myself, Mejirogawa, Haruto, Tsumashina, and Ms. Suzue.

Arriving a little late on account of being on her way home from work, Ms. Suzue looked as if she was in a good mood. "Sorry for being late. But this hall is as impressive as I've heard. I can't believe there's even a reception desk. I went to an all-girls high school that had some joint assemblies here at Seijou Academy, so I've been in the school building two or three times. It brings back memories." She smiled nostalgically.

Mejirogawa looked nervous.

He had apparently been the first to arrive, and when I turned up, he approached me. "What do I do?" he asked. "I can't stop shaking!"

His hands were trembling violently, but I handed him an old, weighty hardcover book and reassured him. "It's all right. Today, the woman you have always loved will be right beside you, cheering you on."

He responded, "Yeah, that's right."

He relaxed, and his hands stopped shaking.

"Sir Mejirogawa, it's been a while. Please just be the same Sir Mejirogawa you always are when turning my pages in your own home."

Surge spoke to him with grace and kindness.

As soon as everyone took their seats in the folding chairs we had set up, we began the reading.

I was acting as the master of ceremonies.

"The story we're going to read today is Kyōka Izumi's 'The Surgery Room.' It's a masterpiece, studded with vivid words as captivating as precious jewels and written in a unique literary style that flows like a coursing river. I hope you enjoy this tale of restraint and obsession."

Everyone had a photocopy of the "The Surgery Room" in hand. Mejirogawa held Surge on his lap, anxious and sitting up straight as a board.

"I'll ask you each to read two pages apiece," I continued. "I'll start us off."

"The surgery was to take place at a certain hospital in the Tokyo suburbs, and the Countess Kifune was the patient on whom my dear friend Doctor Takamine was to perform the operation. Driven by curiosity, I imposed upon Takamine to allow me to attend. In order to present my case as strongly as possible, I concocted an argument about my being an artist and why seeing the surgery would be useful to me."

The doctor, Takamine, is to perform surgery on the beautiful Countess Kifune. Stretched out on the operating table and dressed in a clean white silk robe, the countess looks pure and noble and lovely as she entreats the nurses to perform the surgery without using any anesthetic.

"'I've been keeping a secret in my heart. And now I'm afraid the medication will make me reveal it. If I can't be treated without an anesthetic, then I refuse to have the operation. Please, leave me alone!'"

She fears that if they administer anesthetic, she might give voice to the secret locked away in the depths of her heart. Since it weighs so heavily on her mind, she is certain she would let it slip.

And so, she refuses the medicine.

The role of reader passed from me to Haruto, then to Tsumashina.

Haruto's reading was showy and had a sense of depth, while Tsumashina's was cold and dignified. Depending on the reader, the lines of "The Surgery Room" were imbued with a gorgeous sensuality or a noble strength.

* * *

"'Madame, your illness is not trivial. We will have to cut through muscle and shave the bone. If you could only bear with us for a short while.'

The operation was clearly beyond the endurance of any normal human being, yet the countess appeared unshaken. 'I'm well aware of that. But I don't care, not in the least.'"

Her husband, the count, tries to persuade his wife to use the anesthetic, and even threatens to drag their young daughter in to make her change her mind. Even so, the countess begs him to keep their daughter away and repeats her desire for the doctor to perform the surgery without anesthetic.

Tsumashina finished reading, and next it was Ms. Suzue's turn.

Her graceful, tender voice spilled out softly from her pink lips.

"Takamine, now transformed into a sacred, all-powerful being…

"…'Yes,' she answered with a single word, her ashen cheeks suddenly flushing crimson. The countess gazed directly at Takamine, oblivious to the knife now poised over her naked breast."

The reading flowed elegantly, sparkling cleanly like the murmurings of a clear river.

Mejirogawa stared ardently at Ms. Suzue, as if reliving the day he first laid eyes on her and first heard her voice.

He had sat curled up on a folding chair, surrounded by adults, and listened with all his young heart to a beautiful older girl reading the breathtaking prose of a complex, sensual text.

In her delicate hands, she had held the thick, heavy hardcover.

"A red winter plum fallen to the snow, the smooth trickle of blood flowed down her chest and soaked into her white gown. The countess' cheeks returned to their pallid hue, but her composure seemed complete."

* * *

At last, Dr. Takamine begins the surgery without any anesthetic. He calmly opens up the countess's pale body with his scalpel.

The countess endures the pain.

As she read out the breathtaking scene, Ms. Suzue's face clenched. It seemed as though she, too, was enduring the countess's agony.

Mejirogawa was still just staring at her.

He stared at her with all the pure surprise and deep emotion of the day they'd first met.

He stared at her with all the happiness and heartache he had felt since their reunion.

He kept staring, still hiding the one sentiment that was clearly in his heart—

The surgery continues, and the scalpel strikes bone.

For the first time, the countess makes a small gasp. She suddenly sits up and grasps Takamine's right hand, the one holding the scalpel, in both arms.

"'Are you in pain?' he asked.

"'No. Because it's you. You!'"

Ms. Suzue was frowning painfully.

She read the countess's words aloud almost in a whisper, and the intensity of the fictional woman's hidden emotions filled her quiet voice.

The countess gazes at Takamine and speaks.

"'But you couldn't have known.'"

Ms. Suzue shouted these words, filled with a flood of emotions.

They echoed around the room before fading into silence.

Haruto and Tsumashina looked as if their breath had been taken away.

Mejirogawa was frowning just as intensely as Ms. Suzue, as if he might break into tears.

Countess Kifune puts her hand on Takamine's and plunges the scalpel deep into her own body, just below the breast. The doctor's previous composure shatters, and he goes pale.

"...'I haven't forgotten!'

"His voice, his breath, his handsome figure..."

Mejirogawa stared at Ms. Suzue, taking in her voice, her breath, her handsome figure, still looking as if he might cry.

"A smile of innocent joy came to the countess' face. She released Takamine's hand and fell back on her pillow as the color faded from her lips.

"At that moment, the two of them were absolutely alone, oblivious to earth and heaven and the existence of another soul."

Ms. Suzue's section had finished.

Perhaps she had gone too far into Kyōka's world; she looked dazed, with pain still lining her face.

Next, it was Mejirogawa's turn to read the ending.

"Sir Mejirogawa, please, we'll do it together."

Surge, in his hands, whispered this to him.

Still pale, Mejirogawa straightened up once more.

This was a story he had read again and again, in autumn, in winter, in spring, and in summer, alone in his one-bedroom apartment while thinking of Ms. Suzue.

And now he would read it aloud in front of his beloved.

He would read, together with the kind book who loved him.

* * *

"—Nine Years Earlier

"...Takamine, a medical school student..."

At this point in the narrative, the story shifts to a scene set in the past. A snapshot from when the doctor, Takamine, was a medical student. As he and his friend are strolling through a botanical garden, they notice a group of showy people.

"He is a coachman for a noble family. Three women follow, each carrying a parasol, and then comes a second coachman, dressed like the first. We can hear the smooth, crisp rustle of silk as they approach. Takamine's head turns and follows them as they pass by."

Takamine is enchanted by one of the young ladies in that group of three.

And that young lady, beautiful enough to make even the azaleas in full bloom seem to lose their color, later becomes a countess.

"'Not even the way they moved? It was as if their feet didn't touch the ground. They drifted along in a mist.'"

Mejirogawa's voice grew more intense, and his cheeks flushed slightly again.

Just like a person who had fallen in love with something inexpressibly beautiful.

Surge's graceful, gentle voice shadowed his, as if they were reading in unison from the same book.

"'Now I know what's so special about the way a woman walks in a kimono. Those three were a breed apart. They were completely at home in elegant society. How could common trash ever try to imitate them?'"

Takamine listens quietly to the two young men's high praise of the ladies, occasionally chiming in with a word or two to his companion. Though he acts calm on the outside, the young lady who had seemed like a celestial maiden has captured his heart.

Captivated, just like the young Mejirogawa, whose heart had been stolen by a beautiful older girl, a college student reading "The Surgery Room" in her lovely, polished voice.

With her beautiful face still turned away from Mejirogawa, the woman he adored lowered her gaze to the text.

"It has made me a very happy book indeed to be able to read with you like this, Sir Mejirogawa, our voices overlapping."

Subdued delight filled Surge's whispers.

There was no way Mejirogawa could hear Surge's voice, but almost as if her words somehow supported him, his own voice neither wavered nor paused, nor did he speed along anxiously. With quiet sincerity, it flowed through the room.

"I see, far across the park, gliding through the shade of a large camphor tree, a flutter of lavender silk.

"Outside the park gates stands a large carriage, fitted with frosted glass windows and being drawn by two fine horses. Three coachmen are resting beside it."

Nine years later—

Takamine meets the young lady again.

Up until this point, he hadn't breathed a single word about the countess to anyone.

Despite his age and social status, this man, who ordinarily would have married by then, has remained a bachelor, and he has lived a diligent life free of vice after his school days were over. His behavior suggests there might have been someone in his heart.

We headed into the ending of the story.

"But I have already said enough.

* * *

"Although their graves are in different places—one in the hills of Aoyama, one downtown in Yanaka—the countess and Doctor Takamine died together, one after the other, on the same day.

"Religious thinkers of the world, I pose this question to you. Should these two lovers be found guilty and denied entrance into heaven?"

The countess and the doctor—these two people both holding the same secret in their hearts—die that very day of their one and only rendezvous in the operating room.

When Mejirogawa finished reading the final sentence, Surge let out a surreptitious sigh. It mingled with Mejirogawa's own sigh of relief as he closed the cover of the book gingerly and sympathetically.

After the reading, I asked each person to share their impressions of the book.

Haruto went first. "I think this is a story that could only have been written in a time period when it was much more difficult to marry someone of a different social class and when attitudes toward adultery were much stricter. It's hard to imagine someone with modern sensibilities continuing to pine until death for someone they simply crossed paths with once. It made me realize that such passionate love must have existed back then, too. I feel a little envious of them for getting to meet the person they had been longing for ardently."

Tsumashina, on the other hand, was rather unsparing. "I think the countess's conduct was horrifying and selfish. She had a husband and a small child, didn't she? And yet, she stabbed herself in the chest. She wasn't thinking of her family, and she wasn't thinking of Takamine by dragging him into it all. Even he was shocked by what she did. It haunted him so much that he wanted to die!"

Ms. Suzue calmly concurred, "That's right. Countess Kifune was selfish." She continued, "But I think maybe that was her only option. She had probably been frightened and conflicted ever since learning that she was suffering from a major illness and might not survive, and she was worried that the feelings she had suppressed for so long might come spilling out. And when her feelings exploded in that operating room, the moment she exchanged words with Takamine, she decided to grab his hand and thrust the scalpel into her own breast… I think she did it not because she wanted to die happily at the hands of the person she loved, but so that she could use her death to protect her secret to the very end. To protect her dignity as a wife and mother, and her noble status as Countess Kifune."

"I see. Of course a librarian would have a deeper reading," Tsumashina said with embarrassment.

"Not at all. Everyone has their own interpretation when they read a book," Ms. Suzue replied kindly.

Next was Mejirogawa.

"I—"

Still gripping the thick hardcover book sitting in his lap, he stared at Ms. Suzue and began speaking fervently.

"Ten years ago, I— When I was in the fourth grade, that is, I first encountered this text. I had inadvertently slipped into a public reading at the library, where a college girl with a beautiful voice was reading Kyōka Izumi's 'The Surgery Room.'"

Surprise dawned on Ms. Suzue's face. Her gaze met Mejirogawa's, and his eyes flared with even more passion.

I had advised him this whole time that he should keep his confession light and cheerful. The more serious he was, the more he would burden her, I'd assured him. But there was no way to casually divulge ten years' worth of emotion.

"I was only an elementary schooler, so the story was difficult for me, and I didn't really understand it. But the beautiful words that the older girl read seemed to flow into me, sparkling like jewels, and my heart pounded with excitement. That was my first love."

* * *

This is good, I thought.

Ms. Suzue was transfixed, her eyes still open wide.

Confusion written all over her face, she seemed at a loss for what to do.

"After the public reading had ended, the college girl came over to talk to me. She told me to try reading the story again when I was older. She told me it was an amazing work, her favorite short story."

"Okay, I'll read it. I'll definitely read it."

The young boy had nodded over and over.

"I'm happy to hear that."

He told us how the older girl had smiled at him.

How that pure smile of hers remained eternally in his heart and that, when he reunited with her at the library last fall, his chest seemed on the verge of bursting.

How he had borrowed the same book she had read to him and pored over it obsessively, checking out that same volume every other week.

I had made sure to disclose what I knew about Mejirogawa to Haruto and Tsumashina before the meeting, so the two of them listened to this confession ten years in the making as if it was nothing out of the ordinary.

Meanwhile, Surge commented quietly as she listened.

"Oh...yes...Sir Mejirogawa... I see—that's how it was. Oh...I am very happy. I am quite gratified."

Ms. Suzue still wore an expression of surprise, her eyes fixed on Mejirogawa.

"And that older girl, my first love, was—you, Ms. Suzue."

At last, Mejirogawa gave voice to the words he had been concealing.

She narrowed her eyes and pursed her lips tightly.

"Ms. Fumina Suzue, I have always liked you. I was planning to keep it a secret like Countess Kifune, but now that you're getting married and I don't have a chance anymore, I wanted to tell you my feelings and get my heart broken properly."

He took Surge off his lap and set her in his chair as he stood up. Mejirogawa then pulled a lovely white bouquet from a paper bag he'd been keeping hidden behind him. He bowed dramatically and held the flowers out to Ms. Suzue with both hands.

"Thank you for today. And congratulations on your marriage!"

Tears welled up in Ms. Suzue's eyes as she stared at the bouquet.

Finally, her mouth relaxed into a smile.

"Thank you. That makes me happy."

"I'm happy to hear it."

She extended both slender hands to accept the bouquet, brought it to her cheek, and looked up with a beaming smile.

Mejirogawa trembled with relief and joy when he saw her expression.

"So the elementary school boy who was at that reading turned out to be you," she said. "Thank you for reading 'The Surgery Room' again, like you promised back then. And these flowers are the best wedding present I could ask for."

In that moment, her face lit up as if she were a bride in a church, wrapped in the blessings of her loved ones.

Mejirogawa also beamed, while Haruto and Tsumashina looked on gently.

"Sir Mejirogawa...how wonderful..."

Surge was pleased, too.

Everyone's faces were bright and sunny.

If everything had concluded there, it would have been a proper happy ending.

No one would have gotten hurt.

No one would have suffered.

It would have remained a beautiful memory in the hearts of Mejirogawa and Ms. Suzue and everyone else watching.

I knew that would be for the best.

But—

"Ms. Suzue, is it okay to end things here? Don't you have something you've been concealing, too, like Takamine and the countess?"

Mejirogawa and the others looked over at me, startled.

Ms. Suzue stared at me in bewilderment.

"What's this all of a sudden, Enoki?"

"I heard something from Mrs. Shimazaki—that you actually hate 'The Surgery Room.' When the story was supposed to be added to the library's recommended summer reading, you spoke against it. You said that it was too difficult for ordinary readers, on top of being immoral, and that you didn't like it."

Mejirogawa gasped and looked at Ms. Suzue. She turned her head to escape his gaze and replied, "Is that what she told you? I do remember telling her that I thought 'The Surgery Room' would be difficult for patrons who weren't accustomed to reading things like that, but—"

"You're right—it was probably a misunderstanding on Mrs. Shimazaki's part. But in either case, you did oppose adding the book to the recommended reading section. Because if other people had started checking it out, Mejirogawa wouldn't have been able to borrow it, right?"

"Huh?" He looked even more confused than before.

"I don't play favorites," Ms. Suzue insisted. "I knew Mejirogawa only as the boy who frequently borrowed that book, and I only vaguely recalled his name."

"But you lent him an umbrella when he got caught in the rain and medicine when he came down with a cold, right?"

Her shoulders hitched in surprise.

"You've got it wrong, Enoki," Mejirogawa cut in. "Mrs. Shimazaki gave me both the umbrella and the cold medicine—"

But I cut him off. "I asked her about that. She told me that it was actually Ms. Suzue who asked her to do both of those things."

"My goodness, I'm surprised Ms. Suzue accepted, seeing as how she hates that book."

Mrs. Shimazaki's remark wasn't the only shocking thing she had revealed that day.

"But I suppose she decided to go because Mejirogawa is participating, hmm? She worries about that boy, you know. Says he reminds her of her little brother.

"Once, when it was raining, she asked me to give him a plastic umbrella that someone forgot here, insisting that no one was using it. And you know what else, when Mejirogawa caught a cold, she wanted me to take him some of her own cold medicine.

"I asked her why she didn't give it to him herself, and she said she was tied up with work."

"The umbrella and the medicine…were from Ms. Suzue?"

Mejirogawa looked confused.

His reaction was only natural. Up until now, Ms. Suzue had not acted particularly familiar with him, nor had she even really gone out of her way to speak to him. I'd thought the same thing.

"Enoki, was the young man just now an acquaintance of yours?"

"Huh? Um, I just met him a minute ago, but—"

"I see. He always borrows the anthology with 'The Surgery Room,' so I think he probably wanted it."

* * *

Ms. Suzue had called Mejirogawa "young man" when she had asked me about him. As if she didn't even remember his name and didn't think too much of him.

"According to Mrs. Shimazaki, the reason Ms. Suzue worried about Mejirogawa was because he reminded her of her younger brother. If that were true, you would expect her to speak to him in person all the time. But despite always greeting me by name, she never did the same for Mejirogawa. Why is that?"

Ms. Suzue couldn't respond. She squeezed her fists into tight balls and remained silent, in apparent distress. That was answer enough.

"It's because you harbored a special affection for Mejirogawa, didn't you? You were embarrassed by it, so you intentionally pretended to have nothing to do with him. Am I wrong?"

Finally, she motioned to speak, with tearful eyes that entreated me not to utter one word more. "Yes, you've misunderstood," she insisted in a pained voice. "Today was the first time I had ever heard about meeting Mejirogawa back when he was an elementary school student."

I wonder, if I shut my mouth now, would everything be totally settled?

No! This is just like the scene where Countess Kifune blurts out her secret, which shakes Dr. Takamine so much that he has to abandon the surgery and confess his feelings. Ms. Suzue's wavering voice and fraught demeanor have unveiled her true feelings to Mejirogawa.

The time for a happy ending where everyone got to leave the stage wearing a sunny smile had long since passed.

I dropped the final bomb.

"Do you remember when Mejirogawa's friend, the underclassman Ayuhara, borrowed this book? Ayuhara probably liked him and thought she could get close to him if she borrowed his favorite book. But for some reason, she started to avoid him after that. Do you know why that was, Ms. Suzue?"

"......"

Mejirogawa looked incredulously at Ms. Suzue, who still had her body drawn in and her face pointed toward the ground. "Enoki, what are you talking about?!" he demanded.

"When Ayuhara returned it to the library, Ms. Suzue told her Mejirogawa already had a girlfriend. She claimed that the other girl was a graduate of Yurizono Academy, a real refined young lady."

I could almost hear Ms. Suzue shouting *Stop!*

"Tch, two-timin' jerk."

"There's a girl in a miniskirt, a year behind him in university. He had his arms around her earlier, flirting. A young lady who graduated from Yurizono Academy. Heard they're dating."

I had mistakenly thought the "girl in a miniskirt" and the "young lady from Yurizono Academy" that the book had mentioned were the same person, but they were actually two separate people. Mejirogawa had even said that it was his first time hearing that Ayuhara was a Yurizono graduate.

How had I been so easily misled?

One more bit of information from Mrs. Shimazaki gave me my answer.

"Last year around this time, Ms. Suzue said she wanted to focus on her career, so she wouldn't be getting married for a while. But then, at the start of this year, she suddenly began hunting for a partner, and within six months, she had decided to marry a guy she met on a dating app. I guess that's just how they do things these days.

"You know, Ms. Suzue was a classy young lady, beautiful and refined and a Yurizono graduate to boot. She used to have plenty of admirers."

"The young lady who graduated from Yurizono Academy was you, wasn't it, Ms. Suzue?"

The book that had been so infuriated by Mejirogawa's two-timing overheard what Ms. Suzue told Ayuhara, so he directed his ire at the guy who seemed to be flirting with a younger girl in a miniskirt despite dating a classy lady from Yurizono Academy.

The day prior, I went to the library to set things straight. After keeping sullen and quiet for a while, the book let out a short but audible word of confirmation.

"Yeah."

"Ayuhara had clearly taken a liking to Mejirogawa, so Ms. Suzue made up a fake girlfriend to drive her away. That imaginary girlfriend had an awful lot in common with a certain librarian. Isn't that because, deep down, you wanted to be the one to date him, Ms. Suzue? If you were his girlfriend, then—"

"Stop it!" she shouted, unable to bear any more. She covered her ears and shook her head side to side. "Please stop. I'm getting married next month! We've already chosen a new home and are ready to move in, and we're holding the ceremony next year. My fiancé is a really good person, and my parents are happy I'm marrying him. So stop this," she begged, in a voice that threatened to crack.

"...Apparently, you met your future husband six months ago on a dating app... Prior to that, you said you weren't interested in getting married for a while, so why did you have to find someone to marry so suddenly, Ms. Suzue?"

She appeared to be crying. Her voice crawled from her lips as she hung her head, shaking her shoulders and hiccupping all the while. "I...I realized I'm not young anymore. I'll be thirty-two next month...and I want children...so if I don't get married now..."

"You didn't think you had time to date a college student, right?"

"*...Hic.*" She hiccupped again.

Her affections toward Mejirogawa had already been completely exposed, laid bare for all to see. Yet, she still couldn't bring herself to admit it decisively and instead ranted as if she were vomiting up an ugly mess of emotions. "That's only natural isn't it...? There's no way that I, a thirty-two-year-old woman, could date a college boy... I can't do it. We're twelve years apart, and he's got to go to school for two more years and then find a job. By the time he could get married, I would be even older than I am now—I'd be an old maid. He's headed into a crucial part of his life, a wonderful time when you really shine, and to have a worn-out old woman by his side would be…"

And that's why Ms. Suzue had sealed away her romantic feelings for him. Because a college student twelve years her junior was not a partner with whom she felt she shared a future.

Although she had probably noticed Mejirogawa's passionate glances and felt a thrill of happiness and a flutter of excitement in turn, she hadn't let those feelings show and dutifully kept her secret.

Ms. Suzue is attractive, well-kept, and kind, so I can easily understand how meeting her again rekindled Mejirogawa's feelings of love.

But to an adult woman, the difference between her and a twenty-year-old probably seems more insurmountable than even we teenagers can fathom. Especially when she's the older one.

Ms. Suzue dropped the bouquet Mejirogawa had given her, and white flower petals scattered across the floor. She put her hands over her face and sobbed.

The room that had been overflowing with a celebratory mood until just a moment ago sank into a gloomy silence. Both Haruto's and Tsumashina's faces were stony.

Haruto looked on in pity, while Tsumashina scowled as though she was angry at me.

Heartbroken, Mejirogawa asked hoarsely, "…So you thought that because I was a twenty-year-old college student…we couldn't be together…?"

"…Y-you probably thought I was some horrible, unpleasant hag… You probably hated me…" As she wept, Ms. Suzue whispered in a vanishingly quiet voice.

Mejirogawa's face warped into more and more anguished expressions.

Surely Ms. Suzue had wanted to leave Mejirogawa with a beautiful memory. But her selfish and ugly side had been exposed, and that idyllic hope had fallen to pieces.

As for Mejirogawa, I was sure he was disappointed to glimpse the actual woman behind the pure, graceful, idealized image of the Ms. Suzue he had maintained in his mind.

Everyone was suffering, and everyone ended up miserable.

Maybe this wasn't the right thing to do.

Just then, as I was seized by dark regret, the sound of a graceful, kind voice suddenly reached my ear.

"So Sir Mejirogawa...doesn't like me anymore...?"

Her question was not a servile entreaty, nor an emotional interjection. It wasn't hopelessly masochistic. It was a gentle and graceful inquiry. One meant to soothe a chaotic heart, scoop fragments of truth from within it, and make him aware of their sparkle…

In a voice Mejirogawa couldn't hear.

But as the kind book spoke to him in her reserved way, he moved.

He picked up the bouquet that had fallen on the floor, got down on his knees in front of Ms. Suzue, and called out serenely:

"Ms. Suzue, I—I will absolutely never forget the beautiful words and memories you have given me. This probably doesn't mean much coming from me, but I love you. I have always loved you."

"That's right... Sir Mejirogawa has always loved Lady Suzue. That's who he thought of as he tenderly turned my pages, poring over every word and sighing happily."

"I've had these feelings for you for ten years now."

"He thought only of Lady Suzue."

"And ten years from now, or twenty years, or way into the future, I'm sure you'll be the only one for me."

"No matter how many cute girls smiled at him, he was devoted to Lady Suzue. I'm sure that going forward, Sir Mejirogawa will continue to love her."

"Please give your hand in marriage. If you accept, we can go today and enter you into my family register."

* * *

At Mejirogawa's words, Haruto's jaw dropped open, and Tsumashina's eyes goggled.

Even I hadn't foreseen this turn of events.

To think that Mejirogawa, with his social anxiety and nerves, the guy always fretting like a little girl, would skip right over dating and go straight for the proposal!

Ms. Suzue raised her head. Her expression was a soggy mix of anger, sadness, confusion...all these emotions and more.

"How can you say that? I told you, didn't I? I'm getting married next month. That's not only unrealistic, but it's also absurd," she insisted. "Just leave me alone. Don't concern yourself with me anymore."

But he stood his ground. "If it were only me, if my love were unrequited, I could have given up. But now, that's impossible."

"I'll be thirty-two next month."

"And in twelve years, I'll be thirty-two."

"Then I'll be forty-four."

"And I'll still love you."

"I can't. How could I possibly explain it to my fiancé or to my parents?"

Ms. Suzue's insistence was perfectly understandable. Dropping everything to get engaged to a college student would create a mountain of problems, especially for an adult whose marriage was a month away. Just thinking about it was disheartening.

I raised my voice.

"But Ms. Suzue is not yet a married woman."

Mejirogawa and Ms. Suzue turned their heads toward me.

Seized by passion, I forged on. "Countess Kifune and Takamine's love was barred not only by the wall of social standing between them, but also by the countess's marriage and daughter. Death was the only way they could be together. But they might have met a different fate had Takamine overcome the barrier of status and they united before the lady became the count's wife."

That's easier said than done. But—

"What are the walls that stand between Ms. Suzue and Mejirogawa? Age difference? Isn't that something you could join together and overcome before she's someone's wife?" I continued.

"Ms. Suzue—" I looked into her eyes and addressed her, "Mejirogawa is resolved. The rest depends on you. If you love him, I think there's value in trying to make things work."

Her eyes wavered.

She had probably been so desperately focused on keeping the secret hidden in her heart that she had never even imagined what she would do if the two of them could be together.

She had never considered that there might be another path.

Mejirogawa held the bouquet out to her and asked with an earnest look in his eye, "Ms. Suzue, do you remember the little boy who slipped into the public reading?"

Her dainty hands extended falteringly toward him.

And then—

And then, she answered, her eyes filling with tears.

"I haven't forgotten."

Mejirogawa really did make it official and entered Ms. Suzue into his family register.

Two weeks after our reading, Haruto heard the news and said, "Makes me want to get married, too." I couldn't tell if he was joking or serious.

"Huh? What?! Do you have someone to marry?" I asked in a panic.

Haruto smiled mysteriously. "Maybe."

I caught Tsumashina in the hallway during a break and told her, too. She responded with surprise, then pouted. "Really? He really put her in his family register? No way can I completely support what those two are doing. Just think about Ms. Suzue's fiancé, who suddenly had his engagement broken off on him. It would be downright traumatic if he found out she got scooped up by some college kid. And I don't think the marriage itself is going to be all that sweet, either. My own parents used to get along great, but then my dad cheated, and they got divorced," she told me bluntly.

She continued, "But...I guess that sorta love does exist, the kind that throws reason to the wind and all that. I hope they can follow through on it if they're determined to be happy together and accept all the risk that entails."

"Mm, I agree."

The day before, Princess Yonaga and I had visited Surge together.

Returned to the public library after the reading, she had sat quietly in the section where the modern Japanese literature was shelved.

Mejirogawa must have been busy preparing to start his new life with Ms. Suzue. He hadn't visited the library once since that day.

"It's better this way. Sir Mejirogawa has Lady Suzue, so I suppose my role in his life is finished."

Her words were soft and graceful enough to shatter my heart. But she also told us she had a lot of friends here on the shelf, so she wouldn't be lonely.

"Besides, even if Sir Mejirogawa forgets about me, I will always remember him."

"I haven't forgotten."

My throat hitched, and I could feel my eyes growing hot.

Surge was at once Countess Kifune and Dr. Takamine, who had each held on to their devoted love. I was sure she could continue to think of Mejirogawa with tender affection.

Why are books such noble things?

From my pocket, Princess Yonaga shouted as if she couldn't stand it any longer.

"You imbecile! You ought to hurry up and forget all about a cheater like that!"

She carried on with great agitation in her cherubic voice.

"You don't have any reason to pray for the happiness of a man

who chose a human woman! And there's no value in cursing him, either. Just forget him."

I tried to put a stop to her outburst, but she kept repeating "Forget him" like a mournful refrain.

...Surely Princess Yonaga was rooting for Surge's love to prevail. And Princess Yonaga must have made her feelings clear to Surge.

Surge replied with tender gratitude. "Thank you very much for your encouragement. I'm so grateful for everything you've done, Princess Yonaga, Sir Musubu. But I can never forget him."

Princess Yonaga muttered: "...Dummy."

She was probably only being so quiet because she was on the verge of tears.

I had told Surge I would come and see her sometimes. And that I would bring Princess Yonaga, too.

Surge had answered softly, "All right, I'll be waiting."

On the way home, Princess Yonaga, who had been quiet the whole way, spoke up awkwardly from my pocket.

"Musubu...if you ever forget about me and find happiness with another woman...I will absolutely never forgive you. I won't congratulate you. I'll resent you as long as I live...as long as I live, you hear?"

"Yeah..."

"I assure you I'm dead serious. I would bring about disasters and take the whole world down with me..."

"Sure..."

"...Musubu, are you crying?"

I took Princess Yonaga into my arms and embraced her tightly. The feelings I had held back the whole time we were in the library now overflowed, and hot tears streamed down my cheeks.

Surge had requested me to help the person she loved find happiness.

I had fulfilled that request, and she had thanked me.

But, Surge—

What I really wanted to do was to make your love come true.

I wanted to make it so that he could spend his whole life by your side, always touching you and turning your pages.

I am a voice for books, and I fought on your behalf, but you still ended up heartbroken...

"...Princess Yonaga...if I ever seem like I might forget you, if that ever happens...curse me and kill me..."

Through the tears my voice came hoarse and unsteady.

Princess Yonaga turned my words back to me in a voice also choked with tears.

"I'd kill you...without question. I wouldn't hand you over to any other book or person... I would continue resenting you for the rest of my days."

That was her way of saying she would continue loving me her whole life and remember me always.

"Enoki, what's up?" Tsumashina asked me with concern. "You seem kind of depressed. Let me guess—you have some regrets about Ms. Suzue and that dude?"

But I shook my head and answered, "It's not that. It's just... It's hard to get a happy ending where everyone is actually happy... That's all."

Tsumashina sank into thought for a minute, then said dauntlessly, "...It sure is. But even though it might be impossible to make everyone happy in one go, you can probably make them each happy in turn, right?"

She said it bluntly, but her words did cheer me up.

"I see. I suppose that's one way of thinking about it. Yeah, that's really good! That's great, Tsumashina!"

When I smiled at her, for some reason, Tsumashina's face turned red. She looked away from me and muttered, "I'll just go ahead and tell you this... I turned down the second-year who confessed his love to me."

"Huh, why? Wasn't he some hot guy who was in a sports club and popular with the girls?" I was flabbergasted.

She fidgeted nervously. "Maybe it was because of Ms. Suzue, but I thought that if I went out with him even though there's someone else I like, it would just cause trouble down the line. And it would be really awful

toward the other guy, too. Ah, but it really is a shame. Enoki, you'd better make it up to me."

"Why do *I* have to do anything?!"

"You were the one who invited me to that reading, right? Besides… uhhh, well, anyway, this is your fault! You can buy me a chestnut parfait. Let's go!"

"Hey, wait—"

"Musubu…you philanderer…you better not…"

I could hear Princess Yonaga's chilly, cherubic voice from inside my bag.

"Flirting not only with other books, but also with human women… I won't stand for it!"

No, that's not it! I mean, I'm not flirting!

I tried to explain it in my mind as Tsumashina dragged me along by the arm.

Ah, this seems like it's going to be a real bother to sort out after we get back…

As we walked on, I thought carefully about how I could put the little book with the indigo cover, who loved me a little too much, back in a good mood.

PRINCESS YONAGA'S INNER THOUGHTS

If this gets out, I won't ever forgive you!

He's always spending time with other books. I hate it!

<(`^´)>

Cozies up to them real quick, too.

Σ(° Д °;)

He's too sweet to other books.

(ó~ò。)

These days, he's even spending time with human women!
I hate, hate, hate him × 100,000,000.

(#>Д<)/

...I love...love...love him......

(; ^ :)

AFTERWORD

Hello, I'm Mizuki Nomura.

It's been about four years since I've written an afterword. I'm embarrassed to talk so publicly about what I've been doing since then and how I came to publish another book like this, so I'm going to post it stealthily on my blog instead. I'm also going to include a special side story about Haruto and his aunt, otherwise known as "Book Girl," as well as some other stuff, so if you're interested, please check it out. You can find it here: https://note.com/harunosora33.

So then, this story is about a boy who can hear the voices of books and acts as their ally.

Book lovers all have a few that are particularly important or special to them, I think. And I'm sure we've all had the experience of picking up a book we've had in our room since childhood and turning its yellow, battered pages to reread a beloved story. In those moments, it feels as if the book is cuddling up close or cheering you on, doesn't it?

This story was inspired by the notion that maybe our books really are speaking to us, only in voices we humans can't hear. How great would that be?

When I first came up with Musubu, the protagonist, he was a veeery gloomy kid. He was living with a book his missing girlfriend had left behind, and he had given that book her name, that kind of stuff. But gradually, he lightened up and became the Musubu you see now.

Princess Yonaga went the other way—she started as a reasonable girl, but she darkened in reverse proportion to Musubu's lightening. In the scene where she wanted to take a bath, she reminded me of the little princess heroine of *Dress*. Princess Yonaga is probably her reincarnation.

So what's going to happen to this couple, Musubu and Princess Yonaga?

Is true love between a human and a book even a viable concept?

I think it is!

The title story, Kyōka Izumi's "The Surgery Room," also made an appearance in *Book Girl*. I really love it, and I since I went to the trouble of making Tohko's nephew appear in my book, I included it again.

Speaking of Haruto, I have one regret about his character. I wish I hadn't made the characters in his name read as "Haruto." A good 90 percent of you probably read those characters as "Yuuto" initially.

When I first wrote about little baby Haruto in the *Book Girl* series, I never imagined he would appear in a different story. I thought "Yuuto" was so similar to his father's name, Ryuuto, that it might confuse people, so I simply decided to call him Haruto.

What a mistake! I should have named him Yuuto! But now it's too late for regrets. Please just try to remember to read it as "Haruto."

Aside from Famitsu Bunko, Kadokawa's literature division is also going to be offering Musubu books for sale at the same time. The latest Kadokawa volume is titled *The Long, Long Good-Bye of "The Last Bookstore,"* and it's an important story that I really wanted to write. It's set in a bookstore in a certain city in Tohoku, where Musubu is traveling during spring break. The illustrations are courtesy of Miho Takeoka, the same artist working on the Famitsu Bunko books. All her illustrations are so beautifully executed, it almost makes me cry, so please get your hands on both books if you can. It would make me very happy, and I'm sure the books would be happy about it, too.

Then on July 22, Kodansha Taiga is going to publish *Bookshop of Memories: The Fleeting Utakata Books*. It's the story of an unfortunate young man who seems cool but makes his living selling memories. The "exquisite rose" from the *Vampire* series will make a bold reappearance.

Lastly, I'd like to thank you for picking up my first book in four years. I was delighted to receive messages saying you've been waiting for it. I hope you'll be so kind as to read the next one as well.

May 29, 2020 *Mizuki Nomura*

The following works and website are quoted or referenced in this book. *Pippi Longstocking*, Astrid Lindgren, translated by Yuuzou Ootsuka (Iwanami Shoten); *Pippi Longstocking*, Astrid Lindgren, translated by Florence Lamborn (Puffin Modern Classics); "Rashōmon" / "The Nose" / "Yam Gruel" / "The Robbers," Ryūnosuke Akutagawa (Iwanami Shoten); *Rashōmon and Seventeen Other Stories*, Ryūnosuke Akutagawa, translated by Jay Rubin (Penguin Books); *The Story of Fifteen Boys*, Jules Verne, translated by Tatsuzou Nasu (Kodansha); "The Surgery Room" / "The Holy Man of Mount Kōya," Kyōka Izumi (Kadokawa Shoten); "The Surgery Room" in *Japanese Gothic Tales*, Kyōka Izumi, translated by Charles Shirō Inouye (University of Hawai'i Press); http://www2.kokugakuin.ac.jp/letters/nichibun/syoukai/1nichibun/bungaku_yomu.files/bungaku_yomu-dennma.htm

Artist's Afterword

An early sketch of Princess Yonaga. I tried out a *hakama* version of her outfit, too.